# THE NIGHT AFTER DAY ZERO - A PREQUEL

A. RYAN BIGLER

TOP ROW PUBLICATIONS - ARYANBIGLER.COM

Created with Vellum

*For all the people who knew I could do this, even before I did.*

*Thank you Estelle, Ivannia, AJ & Illene*

*For reading this book before it was pretty!*

# PROLOGUE

*Are you the queen?* The thought rolled through the cosmos of her Dreams.

Dr. Lourdes Garcia Smith slept deeply. Her breath was even on the pillow. Her long black hair was streaked with strands of white. She'd triumphed over unimaginable forces to rescue her sanity, her family and her world. Her ally in this uneasy victory had been just as unlikely as the story itself. He was a ten year old Native American boy named Redcloud who had lived 1,000 years ago. Lourdes' training as a scientist and a scholar had been torn wide open, but this was just the beginning.

Lourdes had never considered the power of dreams in determining reality before she had met Redcloud. As her Dreams became real, they had driven her to the edge of madness and back, but her journeys with Redcloud were not over just yet.

Just as Redcloud had lived 1,000 years ago at a place called Chaco Canyon today, he also died there. In the process of his death, Redcloud needed Lourdes' help one last time. They had saved the world together, but the forces that were tearing at it had one more chance. These forces were beings that Redcloud only learned of toward the end of his life. Now Redcloud's only hope was to call on Lourdes once again. Before, the journey started with a Dream that became a Song. Now the Song would become the Dream.

The Song Lourdes heard that night drew her into an even deeper sleep. In that sleep, a face arose as before, a familiar face to Lourdes but older, much older.

*Lourdes?* thought the face of Redcloud as an old man.

*Is that you Redcloud?* thought Lourdes.

*We are betrayed Lourdes.*

*Betrayed? By whom?*

*Too much to explain...* thought Redcloud. *I'm dying, as we all must.*

*Oh no! I'm so sorry!*

*There is no need for sorrow at my death. I am giving my memories to the Great Spirit. My life has been glorious, but the enemy is patient. His moment has come, and I need your help once again!*

*But we defeated the Giant or the Mighty-One. He moved on didn't he?* asked Lourdes.

*We did. He found peace, but there were others who were counting on him to succeed. Others beyond my Uncle, others even beyond the world you know. You must sing a new Song with me!*

*I'll do anything you ask,* Lourdes responded.

*My memories have a momentum of their own. Please stay with me!*

## 1

## A FLASH OF LIGHT AS BRIGHT AS THE SUN: THE DREAMER DREAMS

Whiteness...

*... your hands! ...*

**Carved Jade Vase** Item #:A2679243

...

- Los Alamos Historical Museum

*... Find your hands!*

Uncle's thoughts pierced the symbols. Then I heard his voice singing the Song of Dreams. I found my hands in the background of smooth stone. The dream became The Dream. The Dream Uncle had promised.

This Dream started out bright just like the others, just as Uncle said it would. Once again, I found myself surrounded by mountains shaped like hopelessly enormous bricks standing on end with countless inlaid square crystals. Thousands of eyes staring at each other and into the sky. I had never seen the sky framed with such sharp edges. These bricks were many times taller than the trees at the banks of the river. The ground swarmed with countless people talking in strange tongues, holding on to strange objects, wearing a baffling array of clothes. I could feel as much as hear the high-pitched tap, tap of their shoes on the stone ground as they walked by. If I closed my eyes, I could mistake the taps for rain under a roof. The blanket I wore itched. My body felt dirty on the stone-hard ground as I leaned on the stone wall.

I must have looked like a beggar as several people offered me small square pieces of cloth. I took one out of curiosity. It had gray ink on one side and green ink on the other with many symbols. Some of these symbols were similar to the marks I saw on the whiteness while finding my hands in this Dream. The gray ink had a picture of a man with clothing that was as unfamiliar as the clothing the walkers wore but equally as different. It was black in color. The man wore a strange beard with no mustache. He looked to be a Holy Man from his demeanor, but I had never seen a Holy Man with such short hair. Indeed, as I looked up, I could see very few people with long hair. Did hair grow in this Dream? The people I saw with long hair were women. Some of them had black hair like mine or gray like Uncle's, but some hair was gold, the color of the sun. Some was as red as twilight. Strange, but all Dreams are strange.

*I must commit all of this to memory,* I thought, but memories were difficult to hold onto in a place where nothing made any sense at all. *I must try, and it must be new memories.* I couldn't stand to watch Uncle beat the young House Girl again. It wasn't her fault that the only memories I could recall were the sorcery of the moving boxes and the black marks in the whiteness. He didn't find them nearly as fascinating the second time I told him. Uncle could be stingy in his excitement.

"The people in this dream can move in boxes with

circles attached to them without anyone pushing or pulling the box!" I said to Uncle only yesterday.

"You have told me of this three times already! I need new details, not old ones!" he shouted as he began beating her with his fists. It was not fair that she should bear the burden of my failures, even if she never cried.

*Details. Uncle wants details,* I thought as I looked around. *Everything is made of stone and brick; it must be similar to the Crescent City Uncle describes. Another detail, this place has as many people as an ant hill, and they behave very much like ants. They all seem quite organized in the way that ants are organized. They all walk in straight lines, like ants. They have a tremendous command of fire and can make it glow in many different colors. They seem to favor red, yellow and green as their small fireplaces are constantly changing into those colors. I wonder what kind of wood or rocks they use to make such fire,... but this isn't new. Uncle's already heard this. For the House Girl's sake, something new.*

*Details!*

*They all carry small, thin, crystalline sheets. I'll call them boxed water. They talk into these boxes of water incessantly, but they hardly ever talk to each other. They seem to find these boxes of water very valuable. The boxes also appear to have some kind of magic in them like the river. These people constantly peer into them as though they seek prophecy or guidance from the Spirits. It's a shame I can't take one back with me.*

I didn't think I could explain these boxes in such a way as to save the girl from another beating. I had never been able to do anything in Dreams but report back details and make stars.

*They have an undying love for symbols here. They have them painted everywhere. The symbols seem to be the best details to take back with me. At least I can scratch them onto stone or into the dirt.* I hoped these symbols would satisfy Uncle's needs. I didn't think the House Girl would stay if he beat her again.

*Symbols it is. What am I likely to remember when I wake from the Dream?* I had seen the black symbols in whiteness before, but I was never able to remember them for Uncle. *Colors! I'll work with colors,* I thought as my eyes wandered. *Uncle seemed to enjoy when I told him about the different color fires last time, and all of these symbols seem to use color in some way or other. Let's see...*

*Yes! First symbol, I see a thin metal trunk poking out of the ground like a sickly tree. Its branches and leaves are two sheets of metal crossing one another. The background of the metal sheet is painted green. In the foreground, there are the symbols in white. They are shaped like "South Temple Street." And the other sheet sitting crossways on top has symbols shaped like "Main Street."* I thought this would make Uncle very happy, but I had to find more details I could remember. I had already used green and white.

*Let's try other colors... Yes! Second symbol.* I saw another type of metal sheet. They were attached to the same magical rolling boxes Uncle grew angry about. Each sheet was painted in white in the background. The symbols were painted in a dark blue color, the color of a deep lake. These symbols didn't appear to repeat in any way and the boxes were moving too fast to make them out. *Wait! Wait! They have something in common! I can remember this!* I thought. *They are shaped as, "Utah."* I knew I could remember that!

Another symbol jumped out at me. One of the magical boxes had something painted on its back as it rolled away from me. The background was black crystal, like water at night. The symbols in the foreground were in two colors, pink bordered with blue. The symbols were shaped like, "CONGRATULATIONS CLASS OF 2015!" *Uncle can't help but be pleased with this, but no more lest my memories blur...*

Something changed in the Dream. There was a change of heart. Someone nearby had become my prey, my crop to be harvested.

PAIN!

The pain of prey in my midst. *I must not fail,* I thought, but I had only made stars in familiar Dreams. Uncle had always been there to guide me. I had never made a star in a Dream without him.

PAIN!

Uncle assured me it would be the same. "Stars are the same everywhere, so they are made the same way," he told me.

STABBING PAIN!

My belly, breathing like a panting dog, was nearly ready to make a star. I saw my prey rounding the corner of the street. He glowed as a star would glow. My belly stopped panting and stung as he walked by me. After his glow faded, I could see he looked different from the rest. Part of his glow came from the fact that he had no hair save one rope-like lock that came down over his shoulder. His brown robes gave him the air of a Holy Man or a Seer, but I couldn't be sure in such a strange place. He walked with a smile as he entered through the metal gate attached to the stone wall I found myself leaning on.

As he smiled toward someone behind the wall out of my view, I could feel my belly boil. There was no doubt. This man was about to become a star today.

I rose taking as much care as possible not to reveal my comparative lack of clothing. I walked toward the gate. My prey had just entered ahead of me. I turned to see him. I did not attempt to enter the stone-walled compound. A man with some kind of weapon looked at me intently.

As Uncle had foretold, just behind my prey, there was a grand stone palace with a golden statue playing a long straight horn atop an arrowhead roof of stone. I looked at my prey and began to Sing.

*The body becomes a ball of light...*

As before, my belly began to tighten. As before, I continued singing in the direction of my prey. He stopped walking suddenly while one of his compatriots steadied him from falling. He turned to look at me as all my previous prey had done. As before, I began singing louder with greater intention.

*The light is smashed into a kernel of corn...*

The man's smile turned to terror. He was crushed to the size of burning kernel of corn.

*The light is smashed into a speck of dust,*

*Then in half and half and half again*

*And in half and in half again...*

The last thing I remembered from the Dream was a flash of light as bright as the sun.

...More blackness on white...

*It's happening again? Please tell me it didn't happen again!* Lourdes hadn't meant for her thoughts to shout.

*No, these are my memories,* Redcloud responded.

*But what's the difference? The last time I had this Dream, it happened,* thought Lourdes.

*Yes. But this is a memory for an event that never took place, thanks to you,* thought Redcloud.

*We can't let it happen again,* thought Lourdes.

*No. We can't, but I have to go on this journey or those that tried to make this happen in the first place will try again.*

*How can I help?* asked Lourdes.

*Right now, you can only watch and listen. I'm reliving my life now. It's life that I lived when I made the stars in your world all those years ago. I have to give everything back, even if it only happened for you and me. You must learn to Sing!*

*Sing what?*

*Listen for the Song of Seeing!*

Lourdes felt her consciousness become enveloped in light. She began to her the voice of Redcloud again, but it wasn't the old man. It was the boy she knew too well.

# 2

# THE HOUSE GIRL

I had gotten used to the terror of the flash and the whiteness that followed when waking from Uncle's Dreams. I had gotten used to the instinctive convulsing of my stomach. I had not gotten used to the fact that I could not sit up suddenly in my Dreaming Hut without smacking my forehead against the weave of branches that constituted the roof. Another cut. It was small but with a lot of blood, like all cuts to the head.

"You need to maintain the same discipline you display while Dreaming when you wake. The House Girl is running out of medicine for your cuts," said Uncle when I slid out into the daylight of the mid-morning.

As I stood to exit, holding my forehead, a bee whizzed by on its way to the new purple aster blossoms beneath the tall ponderosa pine tree that helped disguise my Dreaming Hut from those who might see. Uncle scattered some foul-smelling leaves over the top of the hut to disguise it from those who might smell.

"The local mountain lion was killed by a newcomer. This urine should keep the others away. The newcomer came very close as you were Dreaming. It was everything I could do to scare him off without waking you. He is bold but stupid, strong but youthful, like you."

"Thank you again, Uncle."

"You made your prey a star in the holy place of stone like I asked you?"

"Yes, Uncle."

"In the stone palace with the golden statue playing a long straight horn like I asked you?"

"Yes, Uncle. My prey was right next to the stone building with the golden statue atop an arrowhead roof."

"You have done well, Redcloud." He tossed me some old jerky. "You have earned your meat for the day."

"Thank you, Uncle, for your generosity."

We walked silently down toward the riverbank where there was a trail used by all of the local animals in search of water. I took pains to cover my footprints as I walked in order to further hide my Dreaming Hut. Within an hour, we reached the trail that led to Uncle's Stone House.

As we made our way up the ridge along the red dirt trail, I was amazed that a man with such long, gray hair could walk with such silence and swiftness. My Uncle was truly a warrior of the highest order.

When we reached the Stone House, the House Girl ran out to greet us. She never smiled when Uncle was around. She nodded her head quickly as Uncle spoke in her language. While I had managed to learn a few of her words, Uncle made it clear that I was not to speak to her. We communicated mostly through gestures when Uncle went to the Crescent City. It was not wise to disobey Uncle, for he had many spies amongst the animals and the spirits. The only time Uncle had ever beaten me was upon his return from the Crescent City last year when I had attempted to speak to the House Girl.

She seemed a few years older than me. Uncle told me that I was almost ten years old and close to becoming a man. If girls became women at the same time boys became men, then the House Girl must have been very nearly a woman. She had lived with us for as long as I was able to remember, but my distant memories often became confused with Dreams. When all of her bruises were healed, her skin was darker than mine. She kept herself very neat and clean. She had taken the time to make herself a third set of clothing aside from the two sets she made for me. As of the last year, she had stopped wearing two braids on either side of her head and kept her hair in one long, large braid. She wore a tunic made of weaved cotton. It was almost the same as the tunic that Uncle and I wore. There was not much in the way of decoration, but great care was taken to see to the quality of the weave and fabric. I did not know where the House Girl came from, but she had tremendous skill and talent.

Upon Uncle's third command, the House Girl raced inside his Stone House and came back with a pouch of herbs.

"Redcloud," said Uncle, switching to my language. "The House Girl will minister to your hut wounds." I saw a smile curl his lips. It was very rare that Uncle joked about anything.

I sat down at my customary spot near the fire pit in the clearing about twenty paces from the door to the Stone House. The cooking embers rippled as the sun neared its zenith. Uncle went toward the back of the house, and I felt the House Girl's spirit lighten. She filled a small bowl full of water from a gourd near the fire pit. She took a flask, then a handful of herbs from a leather pouch into her palm. After dumping a few drops of blood from the flask onto the herbs, she then dipped her fist with this mixture into the bowl of water and began kneading the mash in her fist to make a poultice for me. When the mash became more solid, she pressed the poultice to my cut forehead.

The sting from the poultice was different this time. The House Girl put her hand on my chest, and I felt a surge of warm energy entering my body. She then reached for my hand and placed it on my forehead to hold the poultice in place. I heard Uncle's voice bark an order from behind the Stone House for the House Girl. She answered in her language and followed him behind the house.

The poultice tingled in my cut as I looked toward the west over a vast desert to see the mountains beyond clouded in mist. I wanted to think of them as snow-capped, but there was no way to see such things from such distances. Uncle's Stone House sat at the top of a ridge that separated the river landscape from the rolling chaparral between the house and the mountains. The ground alternated between red, pink and white colors depending on how high the cliffs were exposed. Anywhere there was level ground, there were cedar and juniper trees. We were nearing the end of the spring when the junipers released yellow clouds that made everyone sneeze. Sometimes I had to place a cloth over my mouth, but the winds had been calm that day.

A sudden gust of wind found me unprepared. I nearly fell over from its power. As I recovered my balance, my eyes were filled with white light. I saw the outline of shadows in this whiteness. There were three figures, one small, the other two were large. I blinked my eyes. The figures clarified to reveal a mother, a father and a young girl. Did I know her? I blinked again to see the family behind our firepit, in the ripples of heat. I blinked again to see the desert and mountains as they were before. One word invaded me. It was not spoken, but it was understood. "Silence!"

"Redcloud!" I heard Uncle's voice from behind the house. "You must drink water and eat some soup. You will not Dream in your Dreaming Hut tonight. You will sleep inside the house."

"Yes, Uncle."

"Does your cut feel better?"

"Yes, Uncle, it does."

"Good. I'm becoming dissatisfied with the House Girl's work as of late. I want you to be careful around her. She's getting older and more distracted. Are you finished with your poultice?"

"I think so."

"Let me see it."

I handed the poultice to Uncle. I felt the cool air on my forehead. Uncle sat and examined the poultice carefully. He smelled it, then held it between his eyes and the sun. He grunted lightly. Seemingly satisfied, he threw the poultice onto the embers, then watched the smoke and steam as the poultice was consumed by the fire. The smoke rose straight up in ringlets. The wind was calm.

"Much can be learned from smoke, Redcloud."

"Yes, Uncle."

We stared in silence for a moment.

"Tell me more details about the place in your Dream. The place you made the star."

"Yes, Uncle. I remember more this time. I used colors to remember symbols."

"Symbols? Go on."

"With your permission, I would like to show you in the sand."

"Continue."

"This is the symbol I remember the most because it had three colors."

I drew out, "CONGRATULATIONS CLASS OF 2015."

Uncle stared in fascination. "Your Dreaming has improved. Do you know what these symbols mean?"

"No, Uncle."

"Hm. You must continue to improve. Symbols always have meaning. Do you have any more?"

"Yes, Uncle."

I drew out "Utah," "South Temple Street," and "Main Street."

"Hm," said Uncle. "These symbols look the same," pointing to "Street". "Do you see?"

"Yes, I see."

"That means they mean the same thing. You must use these similarities to make the meaning of symbols clearer in future Dreams."

"Yes, Uncle."

"What were the colors for these common symbols?"

"They were both etched in white on a green background."

"Were they on the ground?"

"No, Uncle. They were in a... That is, on top of a metal tree."

"A metal tree? These symbols were together?"

"Yes. They sat one on top of the other at the top of a metal tree that grew out of a ground of stone."

"Same colors?"

"Yes, Uncle."

"Same tree?"

"Yes, Uncle."

"YOU MUST LEARN how to use details once you find them, but you have done well. Have you seen anything strange since coming to the house?"

"No, Uncle."

"Did you see anything out of place on the trail back from your Dreaming Hut?"

"No, Un-," Before I could finish the word, he slapped my cheek.

"You're lying. You're either stupid or you think I'm stupid. You didn't see any new tracks, any strange birds?"

"I... I."

He raised his hand to strike me again. I put my hand up to deflect the blow. "If I saw something, I don't remember!"

"Failure of this kind cannot be tolerated. The enemy is always watching. You must maintain your attention at all times!"

"Yes, Uncle. I promise."

"Yes. You do." He paused. "I must offer my apology, Redcloud. I should not have mentioned an enemy."

He stared into the distance. "I accept your apology." I tried to say this without it sounding like a question.

He looked at me, squinting. The pace of his breathing sped suddenly, then diminished. "I will speak only of the Great King in the Crescent City. He is the Chief of all Chiefs, the Mighty-One, and I must not speak or think ill of Him, and neither must you."

"Yes, Uncle."

"I am in a difficult position, Redcloud. The Mighty-One is the most powerful man in the world, and I must allow you to think of Him now, but you must think only in terms of absolute loyalty. He is your Lord and Master. Say it."

"What must I say?"

"Say the Mighty-One is your Lord and Master."

"The Mighty-One is my Lord and Master."

"Swear it!"

"I swear that the Mighty-One is my Lord and Master."

"Good. That is the first thing you think and the first thing you say any time you enter his presence whether you are awake or Dreaming. The Mighty-One senses people's feelings about Him, and He destroys anyone who does not profess in thought and deed that He is their Lord and Master. Do you understand?"

"Yes, Uncle."

"You have never heard otherwise." He looked at me in a way I had never seen before, as though he had been exposed. Then his face hardened back to unreadability.

"I remember why, Uncle."

"Why what?"

"I remember why I must have missed details on the hike back to the house. It was because I didn't want to leave tracks in the animal trail by the river."

His eyes narrowed. Then he looked to the sky and pointed back in the direction we had walked from. "You missed those birds circling."

I peered out to where his finger was pointing. Then I saw them, several vultures circling far into the distance.

"Do you know what that means?" he asked.

"It means something has died."

"You come to the obvious conclusion when you must find meaning in detail. How many vultures do you see?"

I focused my vision. "I see as many as ten, Uncle." I focused more. "No, it's more than that."

"Yes, it is more than that. What does that mean?"

"It means that there is a very large animal dead. Maybe more than one."

"Yes. Not even a mountain lion or a jaguar or even a wolf pack would take the risk of killing more than one animal at a time."

"They would not kill what they could not eat or defend," I said as much to myself as to Uncle.

"The only time an animal would kill what it could not eat is when it is protecting something it cannot move. The Great Spirit also has meaning in its symbols, but you must pay attention to details in order to understand what the Spirit is trying to tell you. I know you are weary, but you will Dream with me tonight in the Stone House. We must see what brought so many birds together because we need more details. For the rest of the day, you will gather firewood."

"Yes, Uncle."

"You must stay within earshot of the house, and you must call me if you see those birds move or anything else unusual."

"Yes, Uncle."

Uncle walked back toward his Medicine Hut. It was hidden in some trees about 300 paces from the entrance to the Stone House. I knew not to disturb him when he was there. Actually, it wasn't wise to disturb Uncle at all. I walked back to the Stone House to fetch a gourd of cool water.

As I entered the house, the shaft of light from the window frame opposite revealed the House Girl standing in the middle of the floor. I didn't see her head until she turned to look upon me. I felt her eyes open, and the vision of the three people returned to me.

*Always silence*, the words emerged in my consciousness, not as thoughts but as feelings. I felt more as though I had been touched than spoken to. I blinked again and the people were gone, but I felt something warm touching my hand. The House Girl pulled me close, then wrapped her arms around me such that our stomachs were touching. She then breathed sharply. As her belly charged into mine, the feeling, *Remember!* charged into me. I felt the same kind of twinge that comes when I sense those who will become stars are near, but she felt nothing like prey. She let go of me, then she stepped to the side, so she could be seen by the light of the doorway. *Remember what?* I thought. She placed her finger to her lips.

I spent the rest of the afternoon gathering the wood Uncle asked for. Most of the fallen wood had been gathered on the side of the Stone House where the fire pit and clearing were situated. That meant I spent most of my time moving through the slopes behind the house and climbing larger trees to break off dead branches. My body tingled as I worked, but my thoughts were blank. When the sun began to set, Uncle called me over to the fire pit.

The House Girl had prepared bowls of boiled cornmeal for us, but she was nowhere in sight. I sat down by the fire. As I was about to begin eating, Uncle reached over and spread some herbs from his pouch into my bowl.

"This is so you can maintain your strength when we investigate tonight. The stone walls of the house can create a different kind of Dreaming. You will need to create a Dreaming Body here in the waking world tonight."

He dropped another handful of the herbs into my bowl. I stirred them in with my wooden spoon. They had a sharp taste I wasn't familiar with. Uncle had given me herbs for

Dreaming before, but the only Dreams I had ever done were in preparation to make stars.

"I will be with you in your Dream tonight. It may become necessary for me to change my form. You will know it is me because I will look at you and shake my head back and forth like this." Uncle demonstrated. "This gesture is not used by any of the animals we are likely to see tonight."

"What form will you adopt, Uncle, so I won't be surprised?"

"I cannot answer that. It depends on what we encounter. I may not need to change at all. Just like you have a talent for making stars, I have a talent for changing my form into animals I have seen in the past. That is why I know what happens when I am not able to be seen."

"Yes Uncle."

"I am telling you this for my purposes only. You are not to share my abilities with anyone you might meet be they in Dreams or the waking world. Do you understand?"

"Yes, Uncle."

"You are swiftly growing into a man, and sometimes men must keep secrets."

"Yes, Uncle."

"Sometimes men must hide things in plain sight, even themselves."

"Yes, Uncle."

"But let me tell you this, boy. No matter how well others have learned to hide, they cannot keep secrets from me, and neither can you."

"Of course not."

"I told you of our Lord and Master, The Great King of the Crescent City, the Chief of all Chiefs."

"I remember Uncle."

"I told you he can sense disloyalty in the hearts of men."

"Yes."

He paused and looked away from the fire and toward me. The flames were reflected in his eyes. "That is not my talent Redcloud. My talent is even more insidious and useful. In addition to changing the form of my Dreaming Body, I can read the thoughts of my fellow men just as surely as I can read yours."

His words began to echo in my head. Uncle must have seen my reaction or perhaps read my thoughts.

"The herbs are taking their effect. Rise with me. We must prepare to Dream."

The last thing I remember seeing was Uncle's extended hand as my hand took hold, and he lifted me to stand.

## 3

# THE PROTECTOR

This Dream started in darkness, unlike the others. I rose to find myself inside of Uncle's Stone House. As I stood, my vision cleared. A shaft of moonlight from the window projected a white box onto the opposite wall. Uncle's shadow darkened the doorway.

"It is time to move, Redcloud. The moon is setting, and you must learn to see in pitch black."

I walked out the door. Uncle grabbed me and turned me around. "Look back inside the house and see our sleeping bodies. Look into the blackness of our shadows."

I looked inside. Initially, I saw nothing but empty blackness. Then, I felt Uncle blow dust into my eyes. I closed them instinctually.

"I will count to three," he said. "You will open your eyes and you will blink three times. After you blink three times, you must open your eyes and look only into the shadows. The moon will set soon. If you look at the moonlight, you will blind yourself. Do you understand?"

"Yes, Uncle. I look only at shadows after the third blink."

"Begin."

I faced the blackness inside the Stone House. Then I blinked once. As my eyes opened, the black had turned to a hazy gray. I blinked again. This time, I saw an outline of myself asleep on the ground next to Uncle's cot. As I blinked the third time, I saw Uncle and myself asleep in perfect clarity. He was in his cot, and I on the floor. I opened my eyes slowly to find the pure whiteness of the waning moonlight many times brighter than the brightest sunlight. The shadows had taken on a clarity I had never experienced before. I saw patterns in the crystals that made up the stone blocks of the Stone House. I felt drawn to their beauty.

Uncle's voice boomed, "As with the other Dreams, your Dreaming Body functions differently than your waking body. You must not indulge. You must only obey."

I felt the sting of his hand on what must have been my shoulder.

"Yes, Uncle."

"Your Dreaming Body can move with tremendous speed and agility when you Dream, but you must act with Will alone. It is not your feet that carry you, but your Will. You will not change form as I will, but you will seem to float, even to fly. You must follow me and only me."

"Yes, Uncle."

As I spoke, Uncle's body turned into an owl. The owl looked at me and shook its head the way Uncle had shown me before. I focused on the owl just as Uncle had told me to. It seemed as though I would run straight into him as he opened his wings and suddenly lifted off the ground. I followed him at an instant.

He flew low among the shadows as the blaze of moonlight set behind the mountains in the distance. I felt myself piercing the landscape. Trees and rocks flew by me at incredible speed. On the occasion that a tree or a boulder was directly in my path, Uncle would shout, "Leap!" in an owl-like voice. All at once, I found myself sailing up to the sky. As I sank back toward the ground, what felt like my foot would touch a branch or even the tip of a tree top to send me sailing once more.

It was joy! I felt I must leap from another tree top. I saw one below. It came so fast that I plunged into the branches. I felt my body beginning to pierce.

"Focus on the sky!" Uncle screeched.

I looked up to see the owl once again as I rocketed through the trees. Just beyond the owl, I saw a star that was more enchanting than any other I had ever seen. I raced past Uncle or the owl, or whatever he was, toward the star. Then I felt the slice of Uncle's chirp rip through my body.

I felt myself falling, plummeting like a raindrop toward the Earth.

"Focus!" Uncle's voice boomed in my consciousness.

My eyes saw the owl as before. It was some distance down and moving in a large circle. It was descending gently. The utter beauty of the circles caused me to float alongside.

"Calm yourself," said Uncle. "Breathe."

Never before had I felt so soothed by him. I felt airy.

"The ground will be coming soon. You need to think of your feet lightly on the ground. Then you will blink and see me as a man."

"Yes, Uncle."

I felt my feet take on weight. I scanned the horizon briefly. I felt a twinge in my belly that caused me to close my eyes. When I opened them, I saw Uncle standing as a shape in the bright darkness.

"Blink again," he said, "and tell me what you see."

I blinked. "I see ... I see blood. It glows with life!"

"Yes. Yes, it does, but you must remain yourself,

Redcloud. Seeing the blood does not mean becoming it. You must allow this Dream to exist on its own terms. You must not change it through your force of Will. Look at me."

I looked at Uncle.

"Look at my hands."

He raised his hands up with his palms facing his chest. I felt myself racing toward them.

"Now look at your own hands!" he shouted. Did he shout in fear?

I looked at my own hands. They also glowed, but they glowed differently than the blood or even Uncle.

"Yes. Your hands exist for their own sake, not for your amusement. Just as I exist for my own sake. If you want Dreaming to become functional, so close to where you sleep, you must accept that all things are Dreaming their own existence for their own sake. You must let them be in their own right."

I looked at Uncle again. His shape was more distinct.

"Now you will blink three times again. Each time you must think, 'The world is itself.' Begin."

I blinked. The world is itself. I blinked. The world is itself. I blinked. The world is itself.

My breathing became calmer, if not exactly measured.

"We are in a clearing," Uncle said. "What do you see?"

I looked about. "I see ... There has been a great slaughter."

"Yes, there has."

"Wolves? What could slaughter so many wolves?"

"Do you remember the conversation we had this afternoon?"

"Yes."

"What did we say?"

"We said animals only kill what they can eat or to protect themselves from others that would eat them."

"Yes, but there was more."

"Yes, there was more." I felt myself spinning. A new feeling was coming over me.

Uncle snapped. "This world is not here for your amusement! Your life depends on what you remember in your Dreams as well as what you remember when you are awake. Now, why would something kill so many?"

"Because ..." The world continued to spin. Uncle walked toward me. As I focused on him, the spinning stopped. "Because it had something to protect that it couldn't move."

"Yes. Yes, something or someone was being protected from these wolves. These wolves are new to this area. I do not recognize their markings or their scent. Now, Redcloud, I need you to see this ground as it is."

I blinked. "The ground is itself," I said. I looked around the ground. I saw wolves' footprints. There were as many as a dozen of them. Then I saw another track. It looked like a mountain lion's track, but much larger.

"I see something. I see a large print ... There is only one."

"Yes, only one. That is all I see as well."

"It looks like an enormous lion ..."

"... It is a jaguar, and a large one at that. I could say it is more than that. More than a jaguar. It is something very powerful and it has something very powerful to protect. If it is our enemy, then we must protect ourselves from it."

"If it is our enemy, Uncle, then why didn't it attack us already?"

"Hm. Yes. It either does not see us as a threat from what it is protecting, or it is protecting us."

"How are these wolves any more dangerous to us than any others?" I asked.

"Yes. More questions than answers. As always." Uncle paused in contemplation. As he moved within his mind, I began to see filaments of starlight within him. I took a breath. The filaments began to emerge as a fire-like substance. I felt Uncle look at me. "It is time to return to our physical bodies, so we can make preparations in the morning."

Uncle's form returned to the ghostly glow I had seen before.

"We will return in the same way we came. Blink your eyes," he said.

I blinked again. When I opened them, I saw Uncle as an owl. He shook his head as he had done before.

"Focus!" he squeaked and flew toward the Stone House. I followed. This time, more smoothly.

I guess I'd call it Dream Leaping because I wasn't really flying like Uncle, but my feet weren't touching the ground either. I kept my focus on Uncle as an owl. Only Uncle, I thought. I saw myself coming closer and closer to the owl.

It squeaked, "You follow too close. Clarify, focus on keeping a constant distance between us!"

Distance, I thought. I veered suddenly away from Uncle. I swung my gaze back to the left to see I was Dream Leaping to the right of Uncle as though I might overtake him.

Distance behind, I thought. Instantly, I saw Uncle in the distance, his broad wings glistening in the starlight, but he was starting to go dim. I wondered if his seeing powder was starting to wear off. Constant distance, I thought again. I felt myself attached to something ahead of me, but I couldn't be sure if it was Uncle because everything went to black. Even the stars stopped shining, yet I moved.

~

The House Girl with her finger to her lips came to me in a vision as I moved. Her face disappeared into daylight as a bird began singing at a rising morning sun. Was it a call to its mate? Was it a warning? Another bird responded. I looked down from the tree where the bird was singing to see a small village of huts. Several cooking fires were burning. I could smell cornmeal boiling. My attention was drawn to a cooking fire being overseen by a man instead of a woman. As the man's face came into view, I recognized him as the man I had seen earlier. The man who had appeared behind the fire. A little girl of about four or five came out of the hut next to the firepit. It looked like ... was it the H...

Just as I was about to form the thought, the House Girl's face overtook the vision with her finger to her lips.

The vision returned when I heard a piercing cry. It was a war-whoop, although I'm not sure how I knew that. I heard dozens more whoops. I saw many axes raised. Then ...

The whoops were replaced with the squeaks of Uncle as the owl. The Stone House was approaching.

"Think of your feet gently on the ground in front of the Stone House," Uncle squeaked.

My feet touched the ground. I saw Uncle standing in the form of a man once again.

"Did you have a vision?"

"A vision?"

"Just now, on our way back to the Stone House."

"Yes, Uncle."

"What was it? What were the details?"

"I remember ... birds, Uncle. They were singing. It was

very short, more sounds than sights. I remember lots of people shouting."

"People?" He held my arms and looked into my eyes intently. "Is that absolutely everything you remember?"

"Uhh ... I remember smelling fire."

"Fire?" He looked away back toward where we had been.

"Fire," he repeated to himself. He squinted. I started to see the filaments of light rushing inside his body again. They disappeared as he turned to face me. "We have a protector, Redcloud, but it doesn't know us."

"I don't understand."

"This protector sees us as a ball of energy instead of as people. It doesn't know the difference between harmless wolves some distance away or a large bear ready to pounce on us or even a Stone House," he said, gesturing toward the Stone House. "That could also protect us."

"Why would we need a protector when I have you, and you have the Mighty-One ?"

"The Mighty-One is about to take over a new world, Redcloud, and you're a part of His glory."

"But why does he need me?"

"Because you have talents that he needs."

"What talents?"

"Your star-making, of course! You can show the Mighty-One a path to the world where you make stars so He can begin his conquest anew! A being as strong as the Mighty-One thirsts for glory, Redcloud. For conquest! He already dominates our world. We must give Him a new world to test His skill and win new glory! That is why He sent us a protector! This protector is mighty as well, but he is not so wise as our King of Kings. This protector doesn't know us."

"I still don't understand, Uncle."

"You will understand as the Mighty-One sees fit. There

will be many changes tomorrow. You must go back to your waking body and rest. I will tell you more in the morning."

"How do I go back to my body?"

"You must think of your breath."

I closed my Dreaming Body's eyes.

"Yes," said Uncle. "Breathe three times."

One breath.

Two breaths.

Three breaths. I felt the black comfort and warmth of my body. The body I had known all my life.

I WAS AWAKENED by a sudden cold wind that blew my blanket off as it swept into the Stone House. I heard footsteps outside. I stood, covered myself with a blanket and walked out of the house. Uncle and the House Girl were both dressed in traveling cloaks. Uncle lowered his hood and pulled the House Girl alongside him.

"I am taking the House Girl to the Crescent City. It is time for her to marry." I heard the breath of tears underneath the hood of the traveling cloak the House Girl wore. "You must make preparations, Redcloud. You must make a barrier of stone around the house, the fire pit and my Medicine Hut, so our protector knows that he needs to defend these places as though they were part of us."

"Stones? How can stones stop such a large animal, Uncle?"

"We don't need to stop it. We need to show the jaguar that this house and the hut are part of what it is protecting. We built a similar barrier around your Dreaming Hut. You need to stay away from your Dreaming Hut until I return. It's too dangerous. Here." Uncle held out a leather pouch.

"Make some tea with these herbs. Then you must drink as much clear water as you are able. After that, you must urinate on all the stones that you place. Remember, they must surround the fire pit, the Stone House and my Medicine Hut. I will bring back another house girl when I return, but you must take over her duties until then. You must remember that even if you are alone, I am still watching you, Redcloud. That jaguar is not your only protector."

"Yes, Uncle." I bowed my head.

He put his hand on the top of my head, then forcefully grabbed the House Girl by the arm and led her down to the path that led to the Crescent City.

"When will you be back, Uncle?"

He turned to face me. "You will see me again at the half-moon. Mind your duties!"

# 4

## ALONE?

After I ate and dressed, I organized my tasks for the day in my mind. I had two changes of clothes, tunics and loincloths. I found two large leather bags full of cornmeal. I'd never seen that much at once. I guess Uncle wanted me to focus on the barrier instead of grinding corn, which was women's work anyway. That meant I could concentrate on building my barrier today, but I would have to clean my tunic tomorrow as I had only two. That was also women's work, but if there were no women, it became my work.

I started by walking a perimeter around the Stone House and Uncle's Medicine Hut. The Stone House was enclosed on all three sides that did not face the river by a series of arroyos and ridges. I had already walked many of the ridges to the south, so I filled a gourd with water and started there.

Once on top of a ridge to the south, I saw the blue sky meeting the rolling desert for what felt like hundreds of days walk, maybe thousands. Only occasionally did the cotton clouds provide contour to the flawless sky. I turned around to see the Stone House just above the ridge about a ten-minute walk away. This was a reasonable place to build a barrier.

The barrier itself would consist of rock towers about halfway up the height of my knee every two to three hundred paces with a token line of rocks in between. Like the barrier around my Dreaming Hut, it would be recognizable to anyone who knew what to look for but was unobtrusive enough to avoid being spotted by "careless wanderers," as Uncle called them. I'd never seen any, but he assured me they would come someday. Mostly it would remind me where to pee after I drank the tea.

I continued this process for the next two days, occasionally going back to the river to replenish my gourd. The work made the days seem to pass quickly.

The ridges were more uneven toward the north of the Stone House, so progress was slower. The nature of the vegetation also made my line-of-sight marker strategy less effective. I found myself either having to clear branches or stack my rocks higher.

IT WAS NEARING sunset when I came to the top of the ridge due north of the Stone House. The ridge made a natural trail back to the house that I had never noticed before. Uncle always made it clear I was not to walk or play in this direction. I looked at the path to see what must have been the House Girl's footprints alongside that of Uncle's. The footprints were fairly distinct where I was standing, all the way back to the house where the trail was disrupted by a piñon tree. I turned around to see that the tracks led back to another piñon tree growing out of the top of the ridge. It seemed a bit out of place. Even though it was time to go back and start the evening duties, I felt compelled to follow the footprints away from the house.

As I walked, I tried to backfill the prints that were already made as it seemed I wasn't supposed to know about this place. The House Girl's prints were almost the same size as my own. It seemed that the House Girl was resisting Uncle as her footprints were irregular compared with Uncle's. I had never seen her resist him. I continued following the path down as the sky grew darker and darker. My eye caught the Evening Star just as I saw a flash of light come up from the ground in the foliage to the side of the trail. I stepped through to see the wreckage of a small hut. It looked as though it wasn't much larger than the Dreaming Hut I used, but another flash of light interrupted the investigation. I looked down to the left to see a rock glowing on the ground. It was about the size of my fist. I reached down to look at it more closely. I touched it with my finger. It was cool to the touch, so I picked it up.

All at once, I felt myself lying on the ground. My eyes became filled with a sea of white.

A blurred shadow turned into Uncle. I looked down to see hands that were not mine drop the rock that I had just picked up. I felt my belly tighten, and I looked over to see the same Dreaming Hut that I saw destroyed earlier, unmolested. I was Dreaming as the H ...

Again, the image of the House Girl with her finger to her lips flooded my mind's eye.

I was seeing the past. The Vision/Dream returned. I saw her hands grinding dried corn into meal. I felt a sense of relief because I had never ground corn before. Then I saw another hand in the shape of a fist. It was large. It was Uncle's fist. He was adding herbs to the cornmeal. He watched her scrape the meal into a bag. She placed the bag next to another, older leather bag. Uncle gave her two bowls. In one, he watched her place the meal from the bag with the herbs in it. In the other, he watched her place the meal from the older bag that he didn't add anything to. She carried the two bowls down the path I had just found. He watched her take boiling water from the cooking fire and mix the meal. I watched her serve the meal with the herbs to me and the meal without the herbs to Uncle.

A flash of light changed my view.

I saw her hands feverishly grinding more corn and Uncle's fist slowly adding more herbs. One of the bags I found earlier was filled.

Another flash.

More grinding. Uncle's herb-filled fist again. This time I saw a cloth on her hands that was soaked through with blood. Uncle gave her a clean cloth and pointed to a bowl full of water. I felt the sting on the end of her fingers as she washed the blood from them. She then took the clean cloth and continued grinding.

Another flash showed the two bags of meal I found in the Stone House after they left.

Another flash showed her hands grinding again, but it was night. Uncle's fist was gone. She lifted her head. Uncle was gone. I felt the sting again. Another flash, more grinding at night. The ground corn was placed into a third leather bag. Another flash showed this bag of meal concealed inside dirty tunics. The last flash showed the bag being buried with a black stone being placed as a marker.

I FELT a low grumble take over my consciousness as the stone slipped from my hand.

I opened my eyes. It was night. I heard crickets singing.

Then "rrrrr," another low rumble. Two eyes reflecting the sliver crescent moon rose a few paces away. "RRRRR."

It was the Jaguar whose footprint I had seen the night I flew with Uncle. I lay frozen, my breath becoming shallow. It was lying on the other side of the trail. It sniffed the air. I saw it licking its teeth and nose. Then I saw it look right at me and sniff. Finally, it stood and walked toward the river away from the Stone House.

I waited for some time before I moved. I heard nothing but crickets and frogs. I decided to remain lying and scoot slowly along the ground. When I got back to the top of the ridge, I rose to all fours and scanned toward the river. I heard nothing from the big cat. I rose slowly and walked back to the Stone House in a crouched fashion.

Uncle was right. If that cat had wanted to hurt me, I would be dead now. It was either protecting me, or it didn't view me as a threat. It would be strange for the cat not to view me as a threat. I had seen carcasses of mountain lions who had fought. One even tried to kill Uncle, but he was too quick with a knife. He showed me where he cut its throat. We harvested the urine, but I did not think mountain lion urine would matter much to the Jaguar who saw me. He was much larger than any mountain lion.

After I returned to the Stone House, I fell asleep straight away. I felt an odd sense of comfort.

THE NEXT MORNING, I rose with the refreshment only a mystery could bring. I skipped any breakfast and filled one of the gourds. The hike down to the place where the House Girl had washed clothes was flight-like. I saw something new on the ground. It was the footprints of the Jaguar I had seen the previous night. They went down the riverbank. I felt compelled to follow them. As I did, I saw something familiar but unexpected.

It was a rock out of place. It didn't glow like the rock last evening, but it didn't belong there either. I put my gourd down and found a stick that was appropriate for digging. The soil gave way easily. After a short time of digging, I saw it. The vision was real. The House Girl had left me a bag of cornmeal without Uncle's herbs in it. A wave of feeling overtook me. Why would Uncle do this? Why would the House Girl do this? What would I do with the other bags of meal? Should I eat any more jerky? How could I find time to grind corn and build Uncle's barrier? Uncle was not a man to be crossed. If he wanted me to eat certain herbs, then why shouldn't I? I knew I would be punished if I didn't follow his instructions. He told me he'd be watching. How did I know this wasn't a test of my obedience? How did I know I could trust the House Girl's vision?

I took a breath. The House Girl took an awful risk in grinding this corn for me. She must have felt the risk was a worthy one.

I took another breath. Uncle said he wouldn't be back for at least another eight days. This bag had at least five days' worth of cornmeal in it. I decided to use the House Girl's cornmeal for three days. I would dump a corresponding amount of the herbed cornmeal into the river each day. I would also throw a day's worth of jerky into the river every day. If there was no change, I would go back to eating Uncle's food. If there was a change, I would have to add fishing and grinding corn to my duties as well as finishing the barrier and continuing to hope for the good graces of the Jaguar.

I slept in the Stone House for the next two nights. I tried to fish the way I had seen the House Girl do, without success. While I made it part of my routine to throw cornmeal into the river, I had to eat the jerky for meat. I tried to throw it as far away from the shore as possible, but the whole process felt strange. Throwing food away seemed very wasteful. Uncle and the House Girl had brought corn from one of the villages on the way to the Crescent City, but grinding extra corn might alert Uncle that I had not eaten his meal. I had seen the House Girl gathering nuts from the piñon trees. I would also have to add that to my activities.

THE BARRIER PROGRESSED. After I found a rhythm, it became less tiresome. I spent a lot of time thinking about the tea Uncle had left me. If the House Girl ground extra corn to keep me from eating Uncle's herbs in the cornmeal, did that include the tea? If I didn't drink the tea, would Uncle notice? Would the Jaguar notice? The Jaguar didn't seem to be a threat. Maybe it had already accepted the Stone House as part of what it needed to protect. I knew very little of jaguars or their habits. Mountain lions usually napped during the day and came out at night or in the morning, but if the Jaguar was a protector, maybe it behaved differently than other jaguars. Maybe jaguars behaved differently than mountain lions. Maybe it was just passing through and thought me too skinny to eat. Maybe ... I was thinking too much.

As the day passed, I was able to nearly fill a bag of piñon nuts, and I ate them alongside the House Girl's cornmeal that night. At the passing of the third day, there had been no change. I doused the fire to a smolder and went inside the Stone House.

I passed into sleep as on any other night. The darkness

felt the same. The ground was the same. The house was the same. If everything was the same, then why did I feel so different?

I heard the breathing of other people. It seemed quite normal, though I had never heard anyone except Uncle sleep before. Was I Dreaming? I wanted to move, but my body held still. It seemed to be trapped. I started to feel a sense of dread I'd never felt before. I felt myself spinning. At the center of the spin, a point of light appeared. I felt myself moving toward it. It grew larger and larger until I was in daylight, but I was looking at the dirt. I heard voices. The sounds were, at once, familiar and strange.

I felt a hand underneath my arm pull me to stand. It was Uncle's hand. As I stood, I looked forward to see a giant, a man at least twice as tall as Uncle. He stared intently at me. I felt myself avert my eyes. I looked at what were supposed to be my feet, but they were not. They were the House Girl's feet. Is this a memory or a Dream? I felt a shudder in my body and a flash of the House Girl with her finger to her lips again.

"This is your solution, Dreamer?" the large voice said as my perspective scanned my surroundings . I was in a room with stone walls and a stone floor but no roof. This must be the King of Kings.

"Yes, Mighty-One, it is," said Uncle in a voice I had never heard him use before.

"And you are sure this pathetic creature can lead the Star-Talkers?" said the Giant.

"I make no promises, Mighty-One, but I do know the girl to possess a certain talent for intention. I have trained her in the art of Dreaming to move distant objects. She is the last of her clan and last speaker of her language other than myself. It is my belief that her unique skills will make it possible for the collective intent of the Star-Talkers to move the stars and change the fate written in them."

"You are slippery, Shapeshifter. All I sense in her is fear. She is neither loyal nor disloyal. She is neither ally nor foe to you or to me."

"I only wish to live in your everlasting glory, Mighty-One. I live only to serve you. This girl's fear will become the fuel she will need to dazzle the Star-Talkers not only to read the bidding of the stars, but to change it."

"You know the penalty for failure, Shapeshifter?"

"Of course, Mighty-One."

"The moon will shine through the north window in one more cycle."

"Yes, Mighty-One."

"She will be ready to dazzle the Star-Talkers at that time into moving the stars, or you will both suffer for your arrogant assumptions of grandeur."

"Yes, Mighty-One." Uncle bowed and pulled the arm of the House Girl to do the same.

Uncle pulled her out of the open-air chamber. He began talking in the language of the House Girl, which I didn't understand. The confusion ended the Dream of the Giant, but two images leaped from my consciousness to the House Girl's. The first was that of the Jaguar and the second was that of throwing the meal into the river. Afterward, I felt only blackness.

A resolution rose within me. Uncle was no longer to be trusted. I could no longer eat what he gave me unless there was nothing else. Still another. I had to investigate his Medicine Hut without his knowing it.

# 5

## THE MEDICINE HUT

Uncle's Medicine Hut could be easily missed by anyone not looking for it. There was no path to it, so the only footprints around it would be those of animals. Even then, because of his enchantments, only birds or the occasional lizard left tracks. I would have missed it had I not seen him enter it myself. How did Uncle get in without leaving tracks? As I had only about five days left, and I was told to build the barrier around the Medicine Hut as well, I decided to set aside stepping-stones as I hunted for rocks to construct the barrier. I also urinated on the barrier as I went, but I didn't use Uncle's tea herbs, which I also cast into the river. Over the next two days, I had enough stepping-stones set aside to make the journey to and from the hut without leaving footprints.

As I slept that night, my Dreams were more chaotic than they had been when I Dreamed as the House Girl. Falling asleep felt more like falling through consciousness. I saw streaks of images: black markings on white background, hands holding onto whiteness. Finally, I found a cohesive world.

The first Dream started in fire. I heard drums beating and people singing a song that felt familiar, but I didn't remember hearing it before. Then my vision shifted away from the fire back out into the night. The singing grew more pointed, and I saw shadows dancing in the blackness. My perspective shifted again to see the sparks of the fire rising to the sky to join the stars.

What did Uncle and the giant man mean by Star-Talkers? I could understand watching the stars, perhaps even listening to them, but how could you talk to them? What would you say? How would you know they heard you?

I felt myself moving toward the stars and I felt my belly tightening. It was similar to the feeling I had when I made a star earlier. Indeed, I had a vision like this before. I moved closer and closer to the stars. Had I done this with Uncle? I focused on one star, and I felt the weight of it. I felt the pressure, the intense squeezing. It was time to turn away. Any further and I might become a star myself.

This experience caused me to drift back into something altogether different. I didn't feel like I was Dreaming in a new world. I didn't feel like I was having one of the House Girl's visions which were very similar to Uncle's Dreams. No, not this time.

This time I saw the open desert. I had seen this before. I turned to see Uncle, but he was speaking as before. He was not speaking to me in the now. I felt myself squirm in discomfort as though I had an itch or a stinging sensation within my body that there was no way to reach. I knew what he was going to say before he said it.

"You have a gift, Redcloud," he said as he looked out

across the desert. "It is a mighty gift, and I have given it to you. You have been given the gift of making stars."

His words stopped, and I looked at him. I swung my perspective around to see myself. I was smaller. Why did I have a sadness in my eyes?

Another vision crossed my consciousness. I could see myself again, but I was even smaller. I was looking into a pool of water. I felt my small hand reach and touch the water. Just as I touched the water, two other adults appeared behind me. They seemed to smile as they disappeared into the ripples.

No! Who were they?!

But again, my perspective came back to my slightly larger, much sadder self, staring out in the same direction as Uncle into the empty red dirt topped with an ocean of sage and junipers. I was clean but hollow, fed but empty. My mind's gaze came back to Uncle's blade-like eyes.

"In the distance," he said, "you must capture the sleeping doe in your Dreamer's Eye."

I remembered now. This was the Dream when Uncle taught me how to make stars. How could this be new when it should be mine to remember?

I saw my eyes flash open. "I've captured the doe," I said.

"Yes, I can see that," said Uncle. "Now you must squeeze it. You must squeeze this doe until it can no longer be understood as a doe. You must collapse it as the star you visited collapsed you. You must collapse it until it is as small as a kernel of corn. Now sing with me the Song of Collapse, the Song of Star-making."

"Yes, Uncle."

As I began to sing the frenetic Song of Collapse, I could see my belly panting as though I was a dog racing through the forest, but I was standing still. I saw beads of sweat gathering under my hair, the hair of my Dreaming Body. The notes of the Song became more whiteness than voice.

"Yes," said Uncle, "and now you must collapse it until it is as small as a piece of dust floating in the air."

"Yes, Uncle." I continued singing and breathing.

"Now you must collapse it until it is half that size."

"Yes."

"And half that size again!"

"Yes!"

"And half and half and half and half still half again!"

"Yes, Uncle!"

My eyes, the eyes of this smaller Dreaming Body, rolled white, seeing into the back of my head. I fell to the ground, completely drained of strength. Uncle then changed into a mountain lion, starting with his teeth. My perspective spun back into darkness as I heard him growl his dissatisfaction.

THE DARKNESS KEPT SPINNING until I saw a cloaked figure walking away from the Stone House at sunset. I saw Uncle standing next to the figure as he turned around to flash his eyes in my direction. Smoke blew from his mouth to obscure my view, and I felt my eyes clap back into sleep.

As the smoke cleared, I felt a shift in my consciousness. I was no longer in my own mind. Another flash of a finger on feminine lips as everything turned to night. I looked at the hands of the House Girl once more, but they were grasping at sinew, at rolled sinew, a rope! I looked down to see her leg slung over the rope as her body hung upside down. I faced forward. I saw the rope again suspended between trees. As I moved on the rope, I realized that I was on the way to Uncle's Medicine Hut. This must have been one of the House Girl's memories, but how did she get off the rope without leaving prints? Then I saw a small boulder that sat next to the base of the hut. I felt the House Girl's feet lower onto it. She carefully rolled a small rock that held down the flap covering the entrance, then deftly entered.

The floor was dirt, so there was no hiding footprints inside. She reached behind her back, and I felt the weight of a wrapped blanket secured by rope being removed from her back. I saw her hands gently roll the blanket onto the floor of the Hut. Light was sparse except for the shaft coming from the entrance. The House Girl slowly reached passed a stone molcajete used for grinding to find a pouch that appeared long unused. She pulled open the pouch, and a very distinct odor poured out. It began as sweet, then continued to a cream-like fragrance, then became bitter. She lightly pulled a brown-colored piece of root from the pouch. Then she wrapped the pouch and placed a small amount of dirt on it and put it back where it was hidden before with complete precision.

The vision became muddled. There were flashes of grinding and tea drinking alongside the images of the House Girl's village I had seen previously.

THE NEXT THING I heard was the loud call of a crow. Another crow answered. I opened my eyes in relief to see the familiar stone walls of the Stone House. I had slept past dawn. A third called. Then the first responded. I started to hear the sound of other birds. I heard a hummingbird buzzing around the flowers. This must be morning. My visions, my Dreams, perhaps my rememberings must be over for now. A fourth crow brought the sound of familiar and yet vacant footsteps. They were my Uncle's, but he was alone.

I rose to open the elk-skin door. He carried two large

sacks of dried corn on his back as he walked. As he threw down the sacks of corn, Uncle walked out of the house in haste. I rose to look through the doorway. He was walking toward the Medicine Hut. My mind raced through an inventory of potentially misplaced items or other circumstances that might alert him to my new diet or my dialogue with the House Girl. He stayed in the hut for some time. I couldn't take the risk of wandering too freely. I had kept the nuts near the wreckage of the House Girl's hut and taken care to build the barrier away from that sight. I could explain any footprints as stone hunting. My scheming turned into trembling as Uncle came walking back toward the house with arrow-like purpose.

"We must Dream tonight," he said without looking at me as he passed the doorway.

# 6

## CIRCLES AROUND THE CUBE

I had forgotten how small my Dreaming Hut was after spending so many days in the Stone House. The sun was setting when Uncle said, "Like last time, I will guide you. As I do so, the distance will be great. You may see worlds that you have not seen before. If you enter these worlds, you must feel nothing but silent loyalty for the King of Kings, our Mighty-One, no matter what you see. Is that clear?"

"Yes, Uncle. Are we to make a star again tonight?"

"Yes, just like before. In fact, this star should be even easier because you will make it in a desert like our own. Now it is time to begin!"

I slid into the hut as Uncle began to sing, but the song was different. At least it seemed so.

Clear your mind, said Uncle's voice in my mind as he continued singing with his waking voice. A great whiteness came over my consciousness as I began to sing my Song of Dreaming alongside Uncle. I saw Uncle walking with the House Girl as I spun through the sky. Then my vision came upon the Crescent City. My senses were filled with its enormity. It stood as tall as ten men and many people came and went. It was every bit as crowded and busy as where I made my previous star, but the people looked like Uncle and me, less ant-like. Am I to make a star in the Crescent City?

No star yet. Utter loyalty, Uncle whispered in my mind.

We then spun into a place I had seen before, but there was no need to falsify my awe. The Giant stood in front of the House Girl berating her as before, but the vision continued after the Giant left. This time I followed Uncle and the House Girl to the lower terraces until I saw her binding ropes removed. She was forced to climb down a ladder as she wept. The ladder appeared to go down to a room that was completely black.

*Loyalty,* Uncle whispered again as my point of view shifted.

I saw through Uncle's eyes as he walked along a path that led away from the Crescent City toward a large bedrock cliff in the distance. The night passed. A new day, and Uncle climbed a path to a cliff face that could only be seen up-close. The path was steep. It required many switchbacks and careful climbing. Uncle looked up to see the cliff face went up the height of dozens of men. As he looked down, the cliff fell even further to the valley below. The path leveled out and widened. Another turn saw the path went underneath a stone archway curving from the upper cliff face to the lower. As he walked underneath the archway, I could see another archway hidden behind the first.

As Uncle passed underneath the first arch, I could see that the two archways were about the height of a man's length apart. It was as though these archways grew out of the cliff face like willow branches and extended down to the ledge of the lower cliff face. The path carved into the cliff edge underneath these arches was also about the width of a man's height. Uncle looked at the cliff face. It had a symbol engraved upon it at the midpoint between the parallel arches. It was shaped like a whirlpool of water. The lines formed a spiral, glowing with spiritual power. The sun shining through the archways created two shadows cutting through the spiral.

Uncle sat down, facing away from the cliff face and sang until nightfall. As the full moon rose, he looked at the shadows on the spiral again. The moon shadows cut through the spiral in a different place. This time the two shadows were very near to framing the spiral without touching it ...

WHITENESS ENVELOPED the scene once more, and I found myself floating over another enormous building, indeed larger than the whole of the Crescent City itself! Below in a massive courtyard, I saw a multitude of people circling a black, box-like building with great energy. They all wore white blankets over their heads and bodies. I began to see these countless hundreds of people as balls of energy. They possessed the spiritual clarity that made them all ideal stars, but I had to choose only one. My spirit suddenly became bound to a tall woman with golden hair strands that had escaped the blanket on her head. She was praying and running in unison with the others. My intense connection with her caused me to begin the Song of Collapse.

I found the midpoint in her energetic form, and I began to sing. She faltered in the circle but kept pace with the frenetic spiritual energy. This large black box must mean a great deal to these people. I swooped down over the crowd until I found myself running behind her singing.

The body becomes a ball of light ... She glowed. I kept her moving in the circle.

The light is smashed to a kernel of corn ... Then she became as small as a kernel of corn.

The light is smashed into a speck of dust ... She became as small as a piece of dust as the glowing intensified, and I became consumed in my Song.

Then in half and half and half, again

And in half and in half, again...

And in half and in half, again...

And in half and in half, again...

And in half and in half, again...

She collapsed into a burst of glorious fire. She became a star!

~

*Where am I? Redcloud heard Lourdes scream into the light.*

*Is this the Song? Where am I? Lourdes repeated.*

*I can't tell you now, Redcloud's thoughts were those of his older self. The Song you heard was the Song of Collapse. It's how I made the stars, but I haven't learned the Song of Seeing yet in my memories. Stay with me. I'm doing everything I can to hide you from the Dark Creatures.*

*Who are the Dark Creatures? Lourdes breath became more hurried in her bed.*

*You'll See them when you learn the Song as I do. Please stay with me and stay silent. I can't let them find you. Not yet ...*

~

I FOUND myself awake in my Dreaming Hut. As I slid out, I saw Uncle smoking from his pipe and staring at the ground with menacing purpose.

"What did you see?" he said. His eyes remained still.

"I made the star over a large black box ..."

"Before that, what did you see?"

"I saw ... I saw a cliff with two archways extended out of the sides like willow branches that fell to the ledge of another cliff face below. You were there. You sang."

"Did you see the second set of shadows? The moon shadows?"

"Yes. I saw them."

"Did you see the symbol? The round symbol?"

"Yes, I did."

"And you felt utter loyalty?"

"I did when I saw the Giant man."

"When did you see Him?"

"I saw Him with you when you were standing before Him with the House Girl."

"Did you see her go down into the room?"

"Yes."

"But you didn't see the Mighty-One, the person who you saw as the Giant, at the cliff with the symbols?"

"No. I saw only you. Was He there?"

"If He was, He did not wish to be seen by you. If that was His purpose, then it was correct, as the Mighty-One is always correct. You have done well here. I saw on my way in that you completed your barrier."

"Yes, Uncle."

"Upon my next journey to the Crescent City, I will bring back a new house girl. Until that time, you must take over her duties. I trust you nearly finished the cornmeal I left you."

"Nearly. Yes."

"Good! Tomorrow you must grind the corn I brought back with me. You will sleep with me in the Stone House."

"Yes, Uncle." We started up the path to the Stone House. After we climbed to the ridge, I asked, "Uncle, did all of those people die when I made the star?"

"It was just a dream, Redcloud. A dream world with dream people."

"What about when you were with the House Girl and the Giant, the Mighty-One, was that a dream as well?"

"That ... That was a special kind of Dream. What you saw is what the Mighty-One wanted you to see. I am only able to Dream with you under his permission. He allows us to travel in Dreams. Never believe otherwise, Redcloud, or your life will be taken from you."

"Yes, Uncle."

## 7

## WOMEN'S WORK

When Uncle woke me, it was still dark.

"Why is it dark? Is it night?" I asked.

"It is before sunrise, and you have new duties to attend to."

I rose and put on my loincloth, tunic and sandals. I wrapped a blanket over my shoulders to ward off the early morning cold.

"Here. Take this." I nearly let fall my blanket as Uncle dropped one of the large bags of dried corn kernels he had carried from the city. He carried the other over his shoulder.

The bag was as heavy as the rocks I had gathered.

Uncle walked fast. "Keep moving! Time is short!"

We walked along the ridge where blackness was giving way to the orange, pink and blue of sunrise. The morning star shone high on the horizon. I paused on the trail.

"Now!" Uncle shouted as he continued toward the west. Watching the sunrise was apparently not an option. Uncle went into his Medicine Hut. He came out a moment later carrying the molcajete I had seen in the House Girl's visions. Although the stone tool appeared heavy, Uncle carried it with great dexterity. The grinding stone itself balanced on the flat surface as he walked the short distance back to the top of the ridge. My heart jumped as Uncle stopped short of the House Girl's Dreaming Hut wreckage. "It is imperative that we start grinding the cornmeal as the sun rises!"

Once on the trail at the top of the ridge, Uncle set down the molcajete with the grinding stone wobbling on its perch at the top of the grinding surface. "Sit here," he commanded. As I obliged, he began singing a song that seemed familiar, but I knew he had never sung it to me personally. While he sang, he pulled an herbal mixture from a pouch he had attached to a belt around his waist. As his hand moved up and down the molcajete and the smell wafted to me, all doubt was erased that the House Girl had sat here on this very spot listening to these very songs as Uncle spread this very herb.

He continued singing as he reached into the bag to pull out a handful of the kernels. He motioned for me to take the stone and grind. I picked it up. It was heavier than it looked. I turned the stone over to spill the mixture of herbs and kernels onto the grinding surface of the molcajete. I pushed the stone down into the mixture and began grinding. My arms and shoulders quickly became exhausted. Uncle had stopped singing.

"Sit on your heels," he ordered. Upon seeing my awkward attempt to bury my knees into the rocky dirt, he said, "Stand!" He then took the blanket from my shoulders and spread it onto the ground so I might kneel and sit on my feet more efficiently.

"Continue," he said.

As I kneeled, then sat on my heels, I felt the bite of the cold. I started grinding again. My arms ached. "Bend at your waist and keep your arms straight!" Uncle barked. "As a warrior, you must learn to use your body with outright efficiency. Whenever gravity can work in your favor, you must use it or risk exhaustion."

While Uncle's advice helped, after an hour of this work, my shoulders were again sore. Uncle would periodically sing and add herbs as he methodically scraped cornmeal into an empty sack he had brought along with the other bag of kernels. The foreboding familiarity of the House Girl's visions had to be banished from my mind lest Uncle read them, but there was something I felt I could ask him about.

WHEN THE BAG of meal was half-full, and the sun was completely visible, Uncle ordered me to stop. He offered his water gourd. "Drink," he said. I gulped down the water. "Now you are beginning to understand why women are so strong but must be made to feel weak. This women's work is important for your training, Redcloud. You are about to make a leap into a larger world."

"Yes, I can feel that. It was very hard to be alone so long," I admitted. "I learned many things as I was making the barrier."

"I'm sure you did."

"Sometimes, as I was going to sleep, I saw things."

"What things? What details did you see?"

"One detail comes to mind now. It was an image that was two images laid on top of each other."

"Those are not details."

"I saw a part of the desert that was flat. The plants were lower and smaller than here where we are now. In one layer, I saw you staring across the desert. At the same time, I saw you holding the hand of a person wearing the same kind of blanket the House Girl wore as you led her away."

"Was it the House Girl?"

"I couldn't tell. The person turned and you blew smoke, and I could not see her." All at once, I felt a blow to the side of my head. The blow was not particularly hard, but the shock and momentum of Uncle's hand caused me to fall sideways onto the ground from my sitting position. Then, he was on his knees above me with his hand to my throat. His eyes seemed to glow. His face was in shadow even though he was facing the sun.

"You ate something besides the cornmeal and jerky I provided, didn't you?" His voice was even and methodical. His grip loosened as though he expected me to respond.

"Yes, Uncle." He gripped again, cutting off my ability to breathe. A breeze caught his long silver hair, making him phantom-like.

"What else did you eat?" he demanded in the same even tone. Again, his grip loosened.

"Seeds ... I found seeds in the piñon trees ..."

His eyes pierced through his dark face. He took his hand off my throat and struck me in the cheek with the back of his hand. "Did I ever ask you to eat those seeds?" he yelled over my coughs without anger.

"No. No, you didn't, Uncle," I said, taking in gulps of air.

"No. Why did I strike you?" said Uncle as the breeze whisked past my ear. Uncle looked out over the horizon, his face returning to sunlight.

"You struck me because ... because I ate the seeds."

"No!" he looked back at me as his eyes flashed. He paused as though expecting me to say more, but his eyes no longer burned.

"You struck me because I ... I was dis ..." a seeming smile winced his cheeks. "... because I was disobedient."

"You were disloyal." He looked away again into the breeze. His eyes seemed to wet in the wind. "Disloyalty and disobedience are different," he said as he looked back at me. "I left you with plenty of food, did I not?"

"Yes, Uncle."

"So much that there is still some cornmeal and jerky left over, yes?"

"Yes, Uncle."

"Had I told you only to eat what I had provided, then it would have been disobedient to eat the seeds, but I never said any such thing. Indeed, it would have been appropriate to be disobedient and eat seeds had you run out of food. That would have at least maintained your loyalty, but what you did showed that you didn't trust that what I left you was sufficient. Have I not provided you with everything you need?"

"Yes, Uncle."

"Your little exercise in grinding this morning is but a tiny taste of what I have provided you." His voice becoming more urgent, he continued, "Do you think that blankets weave themselves? Do you think that stone houses fall from the sky?"

"No, Uncle!"

"This is the very act that would cause the Mighty-One to righteously take your life like so many flies!" he roared. He looked away and closed his eyes. I saw his belly moving in and out of view as he breathed deeply. The sun was becoming warm on my skin.

Uncle stood and scanned the horizon. "You said you saw the House Girl before you made the star in your last Dream."

"Yes, I did."

"What were the circumstances in which you saw her? And you must answer with complete loyalty."

"I saw her standing before the Giant, the Mighty-One, in a room of stone walls with an open sky above. The Giant seemed displeased, but I … I couldn't understand his language."

"Is that all?"

"No. I saw her in one other place. I saw you show her to a ladder that led to a room beneath a floor."

"What else?"

"I saw her go down into a room that was in complete darkness. After that, I saw the city with the people circling the cube."

"She went into darkness."

"With all loyalty, Uncle, that is what I saw in the Dream."

He peered at me a moment. Then he looked at the ground. Then back at me. His face was motionless.

He cleaned the molcajete with a bit of water from his gourd. "You are to grind the rest of this corn and place the meal into these sacks. You are to do it with utter, utter loyalty for your Uncle and your Mighty-One. Is that now completely understood?"

"Yes, Uncle."

With that, he rose. He left behind the water gourd and enough jerky for me to proceed until sundown. It took all of my strength, but I ground the rest of that corn. My thoughts were of utter loyalty. Occasionally, that loyalty was focused on the Giant and Uncle. I couldn't argue with the fact that they had given me all I had. However, my loyalty to the House Girl was now unequivocal.

~

I STAGGERED BACK to find Uncle watching the cooking fire with rapt attention. Without looking at me, he said, "You may sit down in front of the fire, Redcloud, after you place the cornmeal inside the Stone House."

It took all of my remaining strength to place the sack inside the house. When I returned, Uncle had filled a bowl full of cornmeal with a tea he had prepared.

As I sat, Uncle looked at me and said, "I've prepared a tea to soothe you in your new work."

"Thank you, Uncle," I said as I picked up the tea with new skepticism. Doubts were not wise, so I ate and drank in the way I remembered best.

As I drank the tea, I noticed a new flavor. Within a moment, I felt myself fall sideways into Uncle's cold hands. I was asleep.

As I slept, I felt the sting of my breath moving in and out of my chest. My heart pounded like thunder. Was this a Dream? Was it a Vision? Lightning started streaking across the background. I felt my feet suddenly give way, which usually woke me from a Dream, but now, I just kept falling. I felt I was spinning in blackness.

"Utter loyalty!" boomed Uncle.

I felt my body turn to face my stomach toward the ground (or what I sensed to be the ground). The spinning stopped. I saw fire below. I felt fire licking at my skin, but I was powerless to move. I looked down to see I was above a burning hut as though I were a carcass on a spit.

I screamed as I managed to roll my body, so my back was now to the flames.

I rotated once more to find myself out of the flames. I saw people running in all directions.

In the distance, I saw two enormous creatures. They were swinging clubs, hurling many to their fiery deaths. The last thing I remember seeing was Uncle with a baby prostrate before the Giant. I could still see flames in the distance, but the scene with Uncle was removed from the fire.

"Utter loyalty!" Uncle admonished once again.

I felt a surge of questions come upon me, but I had no words to bring them forth.

THE NEXT THING I remember seeing was Uncle's face as it looked down on me when I opened my eyes at what felt like the next morning. Uncle's face came into focus.

"You must now learn to clean clothes," he said.

I got dressed and met Uncle at the fire.

"Drink this tea and eat this jerky, then drink a good amount of water."

"Yes, Uncle," I said.

"There are no magical methods for cleaning clothes," he explained as I ate and drank. "The clothes are only as clean as the work you put in to clean them. Come. I will show you where the House Girl washed before. Bring the bags of laundry."

I picked up the bags. They both had strings through their openings, but there was no way of carrying them without reminding me how hard I worked the previous day. "Make haste!" Uncle shouted. "You must be at least as strong as the House Girl!" He laughed.

Utter loyalty, I thought as I followed Uncle down. I was glad I took the time to brush out the footprints from my previous journeys. Once we arrived, however, there were a number of other prints in the dirt. Uncle stopped to inspect. He bent to the ground and filled his belly full of air. His belly bobbed as I watched him sniff the prints like a coyote.

"Mountain lions have been through here." He sniffed

again. "Their markings are fresh enough for a man's nose to smell them. That means only one or two days." He rose and sniffed the bark of a nearby tree. "Yes, Redcloud. Come and smell this bark. First, inhale through your nose until your belly is full of air, then pant like a wild animal through your nose, and blow out through your mouth away from the bark so you can know this smell."

I did as I was instructed. While Uncle's tea seemed to help, the soreness of my body from grinding corn came roaring back as my stomach muscles flexed and retreated like an animal's. I smelled something resembling the metal in Uncle's bracelet mixed with a smell similar to my own urine.

"Do you smell it?" asked Uncle.

"Yes, Uncle."

"Now, look here." He pointed to the bark. There were pieces of yellow fur caught in the bark of the tree. Uncle leaned in to smell again. "Curious," he said. "There are two. You must be cautious, Redcloud. Keep an eye out as you wash. Cougars are solitary creatures. Two together is strange. This is not usually mating season. Come. I will show you how to wash."

Uncle snatched up one of the bags I had carried and walked over to a boulder that sat next to the riverbank. He pulled out one of my dirty tunics and demonstrated how to dip the cotton tunic into the river, then rub it with a special kind of bark filled with deer fat that made the water bubble up. Then he showed me how to scrub the tunic against the flat boulder until all of the dirt had been removed. Dipping the tunic in the river again, he proceeded to wring all the bubbles out of the cloth. I knew I would not be able to wash clothes as effectively as Uncle, whose competence at everything he did seemed marvelous to me. My admiration grew for the House Girl even more. While I could not allow my thoughts to wander beyond a flicker of an instant, the House Girl's strength and prowess, her beauty, could not be denied.

"Now you."

I picked up one of Uncle's tunics and put it into the shallow pool on the riverbank as Uncle had done. My body was initially shocked at how heavy it became as the water dripped back into the river. I nearly lost my balance.

"Move quickly! Think of it as a dance, and you will keep your balance," Uncle admonished.

I threw the tunic onto the boulder as Uncle had done. I rubbed the bark onto the tunic as pain shot through my body. "As I said yesterday, use your body as a lever, so you don't have to work as hard," said Uncle. I changed my position so I could fall onto the boulder with the bark piece in my hands. This shifted my pain to other parts of my body that I didn't know I had. "Put the bark aside and use one part of the tunic to scrub the dirt out of the other. Then use the boulder to scrub as well," he said. I did my best to follow his instructions. My efforts must have been at least somewhat satisfactory, as he grunted in approval as the bubbles dripped into the pool of water.

"You must wash all the clothes in these bags before sundown. It is not safe to remain here after dark when there are so many big cats around."

"Yes, Uncle."

"I will expect you to clean these two bags of laundry and hang the clothes from the trees like this." He demonstrated. "You must be back before twilight."

"Yes, Uncle."

Uncle walked with his usual urgency back up the trail to the Stone House, and I began my career as a launderer. As I wrung out the second tunic, I felt a simultaneous relief of movement combined with a searing soreness of exhaustion. The sun was still low in the east and the trees would provide plenty of shade throughout the day. I checked the pouch on my belt. Uncle had packed jerky. My ambivalence at eating the food he had provided was easily overcome by my hunger and fatigue. Still, I stopped after finishing one piece.

No time for pity or curiosity, I thought and continued scrubbing, wringing, drying and dipping.

After about five tunics, I lost track of time, and my field of vision became narrow as I worked. My mind and body had never felt so unified. Once again, the image of the House Girl, the hut and the pouch rolled through me. I felt a sense of befuddlement as I attempted to bury thoughts of how I might be able to get into Uncle's hut, let alone his pouch, without being discovered.

I inspected my wet tunic, or was it Uncle's? Dirt was still evident, but when I dipped it back into the river water, most of the dirt was carried away in the pool. As the water babbled back into the river, I heard a low rumbling. I tossed the tunic back onto the washing-boulder and proceeded to roll out the water just as Uncle had demonstrated when I heard the rumble again. I scanned the foliage adjacent to the riverbank. Once again, the rumble. It was not as low or as strangely soothing as the Jaguar's had been. The rumble turned into a growl with a growing sense of menace and aggression.

As I screamed "Uncle," a mountain lion leaped from the bushes just to the right of where I was looking. Its speed and power were shocking as it came for me. My scream seemed to be punctured by its fierce growl. I twisted my body instinctively back and raised my right hand to present a defense, but the cat's claws had already entered my legs. The heel of my palm pushed down on the cat's nose, which kept it from biting into my side and caused its claws to rip down my right leg. My blood began to spill as I saw the cat recoil after having been effectively struck on the nose. I saw dirt on its snout as I registered that I must have pushed it into the ground. The cat sneezed and growled once more.

I felt my consciousness begin to wane when Uncle suddenly appeared. The last thing I remember seeing was Uncle's club smashing up against the cat's snout as another cat leaped toward Uncle's back.

## 8

## THE COUGARS

The blackness was pierced with the sting in my legs. As I drew breath, I felt tears escape both of my eyes, and my lower jaw quivered. My breath caught as I found myself crying. I tried to keep my voice down, but this kind of pain was old pain. I knew I had felt it before, but I couldn't remember where or when, nor did I care.

"Don't catch your breath. Breathe deeply." Uncle's voice ripped through me. "Breathe into your belly," he said. "And don't worry if you faint. Sleeping is the fastest route to healing."

I felt my belly fill with air, and I started to moan.

"You will not be fit until your breathing evens out. Sit up and drink this water."

As I sat, my eyes cleared briefly to reveal the bandages and poultices on my thighs. I drank through the pain. Upon a gulp, the memory rushed back that Uncle had been attacked by a second cat, but that memory was cast aside when I could drink no more and my breath again went back to crying. I felt myself fall backward to lie flat on the floor of the Stone House. The thatched ceiling once again disappearing into tears, pain, and finally blackness.

The next time I awoke, my urge to pee was greater than the pain I felt. "I need to pee," I said to myself. My eyes opened suddenly as I was lifted up by the armpits. When I was able to stand on my own, the top of my head reached Uncle's chin, but his great strength made me feel light. His face was a comfort.

"I will help you to the latrine."

Walking brought tears to my eyes, but I was able to breathe more evenly now.

"How long have I been asleep?"

"Three days," said Uncle.

"How did I survive? I saw a second cougar just as I fell."

"Yes, there was a second cat, but I was able to maneuver so that he was only able to graze my belly before I struck him with my club."

"Did you kill them?"

"No. No, they both escaped into the woods. Their behavior was most unusual. I suspect they'll be back."

After I relieved myself, we walked back to the Stone House. I resumed my spot on the floor. Uncle filled a bowl with some tea, then grabbed a water gourd.

"You must drink the tea slowly. It is bitter, but it will speed your healing process, so you'll be fit to Dream. After you finish the tea, you must drink the water quickly and completely."

"Yes, Uncle."

I sipped the tea. The taste was as disagreeable as it was unfamiliar, but the flavor was at least enough to forget my legs which had gone from sting to ache. A question entered my mind. "How do you know the cougars will return?"

"I'm not sure. Something about their energy gave me the impression they viewed you as their prize."

"Will we have to kill them?"

"It is possible but distasteful. Mountain lions are far more useful alive than dead."

"Why?"

"Because they drive the game out of the mountains, and they kill the weak and unfit. They are not such fools as are we."

I nodded and finished my tea. Uncle handed me the gourd and motioned for me to drink.

"I know you are still in pain, but we must Dream again and make a new star."

I brought the gourd down to ask a question, only to have Uncle say, "You must finish the water!"

I continued to drink until the gourd was empty. He took the gourd as I handed it to him.

"Will we go to my Dreaming Hut?" I asked.

"We don't have a choice," he said. "You are too weak to make a star from anywhere else."

"But what about the cougars?"

"All you need to be concerned with is loyalty. I'll keep you safe as I did before. It is critical for the Mighty-One that you make this star tonight."

"Yes, Uncle."

"For now, you must rest until it's time to go."

"Yes, Uncle."

It was easy to sleep and hard to wake. I never thought of the hike to my Dreaming Hut as difficult, but my pain was punctuated at every uneven step. The soles of my feet became instantly aware of every rock and branch underneath my sandals. We arrived, as usual, at twilight. Uncle helped me to slide into my hut. I heard Uncle singing a new

Song and waving his club as he danced around the periphery of the hut. I felt my breathing take over when I heard the familiar Song of Dreaming rise from his voice. I sang with him ...

THE BLACKNESS WAS PIERCED with the sting in my legs. As I drew breath, I felt tears escape both of my eyes, and my lower jaw quivered. My breath caught as I found myself crying. I tried to keep my voice down, but this kind of pain was old pain. I knew I had felt it before, but I couldn't remember where or when, nor did I care.

"Don't catch your breath. Breathe deeply." Uncle's voice ripped through me. "Breathe into your belly," he said. "And don't worry if you faint. Sleeping is the fastest route to healing."

I felt my belly fill with air, and I started to moan.

"You will not be fit until your breathing evens out. Sit up and drink this water."

As I sat, my eyes cleared briefly to reveal the bandages and poultices on my thighs. I drank through the pain. Upon a gulp, the memory rushed back that Uncle had been attacked by a second cat, but that memory was cast aside when I could drink no more and my breath again went back to crying. I felt myself fall backward to lie flat on the floor of the Stone House. The thatched ceiling once again disappearing into tears, pain, and finally blackness.

The next time I awoke, my urge to pee was greater than the pain I felt. "I need to pee," I said to myself. My eyes opened suddenly as I was lifted up by the armpits. When I was able to stand on my own, the top of my head reached Uncle's chin, but his great strength made me feel light. His face was a comfort.

“I will help you to the latrine.”

Walking brought tears to my eyes, but I was able to breathe more evenly now.

"How long have I been asleep?”

“Three days,” said Uncle.

“How did I survive? I saw a second cougar just as I fell.”

“Yes, there was a second cat, but I was able to maneuver so that he was only able to graze my belly before I struck him with my club.”

“Did you kill them?”

“No. No, they both escaped into the woods. Their behavior was most unusual. I suspect they’ll be back.”

After I relieved myself, we walked back to the Stone House. I resumed my spot on the floor. Uncle filled a bowl with some tea, then grabbed a water gourd.

“You must drink the tea slowly. It is bitter, but it will speed your healing process, so you’ll be fit to Dream. After you finish the tea, you must drink the water quickly and completely.”

“Yes, Uncle.”

I sipped the tea. The taste was as disagreeable as it was unfamiliar, but the flavor was at least enough to forget my legs which had gone from sting to ache. A question entered my mind. “How do you know the cougars will return?”

“I’m not sure. Something about their energy gave me the impression they viewed you as their prize.”

“Will we have to kill them?”

“It is possible but distasteful. Mountain lions are far more useful alive than dead.”

“Why?”

“Because they drive the game out of the mountains, and they kill the weak and unfit. They are not such fools as are we.”

I nodded and finished my tea. Uncle handed me the gourd and motioned for me to drink.

"I know you are still in pain, but we must Dream again and make a new star."

I brought the gourd down to ask a question, only to have Uncle say, "You must finish the water!"

I continued to drink until the gourd was empty. He took the gourd as I handed it to him.

"Will we go to my Dreaming Hut?" I asked.

"We don't have a choice," he said. "You are too weak to make a star from anywhere else."

"But what about the cougars?"

"All you need to be concerned with is loyalty. I'll keep you safe as I did before. It is critical for the Mighty-One that you make this star tonight."

"Yes, Uncle."

"For now, you must rest until it's time to go."

"Yes, Uncle."

It was easy to sleep and hard to wake. I never thought of the hike to my Dreaming Hut as difficult, but my pain was punctuated at every uneven step. The soles of my feet became instantly aware of every rock and branch underneath my sandals. We arrived, as usual, at twilight. Uncle helped me to slide into my hut. I heard Uncle singing a new Song and waving his club as he danced around the periphery of the hut. I felt my breathing take over when I heard the familiar Song of Dreaming rise from his voice. I sang with him ...

ON AN INHALE, I found myself drifting through the sky. As a white cloud passed, I could see another great city. This one was in the desert as well, but instead of seeing a valley surrounded by mountains, I saw a small mountain that dominated a plain full of strange buildings. Some of them looked like the upright metal bricks and crystals of the first city in which I made a star. The buildings next to the mountain looked as though they were made of stone in a similar manner to the Crescent City, with one shiny exception. On top of the highest building on the small mountain in the middle of the city, there was a ball of gold. The base of the building the ball rested upon was eight-sided and appeared to be made out of turquoise. There was a spear at the top of the golden ball with two curved points shooting into the sky. I had never seen such a thing!

As shiny as the golden ball was, my instincts were drawn to a large courtyard of white stone that sat at the base of the small mountain topped by the golden dome. A man in an orange robe radiated the strength and resolve that best suited my star-makers. I felt my arms turn to black wings as I circled my way down to the courtyard.

The courtyard was nearly empty except for a few barriers and men wearing the strange clothing of Uncle's star-making world. Two of them wore red caps and stood like statues. Several other men began to approach me from behind after I landed to resume my human form. I focused all of my attention on the man in the orange robe and began my Song of Collapse just after the man passed the two men who did not move. The man in the robe immediately collapsed and began glowing. I saw many other men dressed in similar clothing approach me, but the slightest inclination of my Song of Collapse caused them to double over in pain.

The man in the robe collapsed to the size of a kernel of corn, then to the size of a piece of dust, then in half, then in half, then in half still again until halving was all that he was, until he ceased to be himself and exploded into the brilliance of a star on Earth!

As I began the journey back to my hut, I felt my legs begin to burn with the heat of that star. My breath quickened and my Song began to change as I felt a wave of immense power push me away.

I'M SCARED. *What is happening to me! I'm still lost,* Lourdes responded in her Dream.

*Please don't leave me!* thought Redcloud. *I'm giving my experience back to the Great Spirit, and the Dark Creatures are waiting.*

*I can't see anything but burning and fire.*

*You can't see them until I learn the Song of Seeing.*

*I can't breathe here. I can't stay, thought Lourdes.*

*Breathe into the fire! Redcloud entreated.*

*I don't understand.*

*Breathe like a dog.*

*Lourdes breath became more measured.*

*Stay with me!* Redcloud begged. The tambour of his thoughts became that of a child again.

WAS I being pushed away from my Dreaming Hut? Was I being pushed away from the man in orange who became the star that devoured the city? That devoured the thousands who lived in the other cities? The cities that shall now be stars? *Am I a star? Am I alive? What am I?*

The world cascaded in heat, in waves. I was adrift. I was alone. I saw fire. I saw hundreds of huts burning. I saw two

Giants smashing the burning huts with their giant clubs. I saw them as two giant skeletons smashing smaller skeletons with distended bones used as clubs. Then I saw them as flesh smashing people of flesh. I saw these people writhing in fire. What passed for my vision began to see the Giants come together, then split apart as flesh, as bones, and as flesh again. I heard the roar of flame. I felt the sting of pain. I opened my eyes to hear the cougars again.

I HEARD the wind of the club swinging as Uncle did unseen battle. His breathing was heavy as I heard bone splinter, a howl of pain, and then the roof of my hut collapsed. I screamed as the blood of one of the cougars ran down my neck, and the weight of the lean, breathing muscle, fur and branches collapsed onto my legs.

SILENCE! Uncle's thought thundered as I heard feet leave the ground, and a fierce growl pierced my consciousness. Then I saw claws rip through the branches of my hut and expose the stars. Another whoosh gave report of Uncle's club as I saw him leap over my field of vision. The other mountain lion growled and hissed again. Uncle leaped across in the opposite direction. It took all of my strength to keep breathing without making sound when I felt the stunned cat on top of me sink even further into my body.

The branches of the roof lowered further until I saw Uncle with his eyes glowing and his face darker than the night sky. He was driving a stake of wood into the body of the cat on top of me. As he jammed it further into the limp body, I heard the panic of the dying mountain lion above my head. Another thrust by Uncle caused one of the branches to pierce my right leg. I began to breathe uncontrollably as the cat on top of me gurgled its last breath. Uncle must have twisted the stake again in t he dead animal when I felt the stake's tip begin to poke at my own abdomen.

Uncle seemed to float off of me as he tossed the cat aside. His eyes continued to glow as he removed the debris from on top of me.

Then Uncle howled a note. I turned my head, and I saw him sleeping on the ground just outside of my hut while at the same time his dark-faced double picked me out of the wreckage with the greatest care. The body that held me was taut and strong. I turned my head to observe Uncle's other body asleep. The sleeping Uncle disappeared as I felt the wind of a tremendous leap into the air, and all I could see was the night sky. Suddenly, trees raced into my vision again as I heard Uncle's feet touch the ground. His breath seemed to have a hollow echo as the stars of the Milky Way rushed downward, and I saw the river racing by in shimmers of darkness. I felt my toes enter the ice-cold water, then my calves, my knees and my ...

## 9

# RECOVERY?

As I awoke, my sensibilities told me I wasn't the only one in pain. I sat up slowly to find a large gourd next to me. There was another propped up against the bed where Uncle slept. It was daylight out. I watched Uncle sleep as I drank the water. Up to this point in my life, I'd never seen Uncle do anything without some kind of purpose behind it. Even on the rare occasions I had seen him sleep, there was always an alertness to his demeanor, but not today. Even in my own exhaustion, I felt a hollowness to his sleep, as though he was spent, an old man. Neither of us was in a position to defend against predatory cougars.

As water sharpened my consciousness, the strangeness of those cougars began to take over my mind. Why would two cougars fight to the death to attack Uncle and me? As Uncle mentioned, cougars were not such fools as we. Either these cougars were such fools, or perhaps they weren't cougars at all. Maybe they were Shapeshifters, but two of them?

The thought of two of anything made me see two of Uncle's gourd and two of everything else. It took all of my remaining energy to put down my own water and resume sleeping.

THE NEXT TIME I AWOKE, Uncle was no longer in his bed. I heard his usual deliberate footsteps outside as he moved about.

Sitting up, I saw that my dressings had been changed and my gourd had been refilled. I looked to the corner to see that Uncle had prepared another sack of cornmeal. My legs still ached, but they felt functional. I pulled myself to standing and got dressed, then moved to the elk-skin door to see a bright, colorful morning. There was still a slight chill. A flicker of fright came over me when I didn't see Uncle.

The cooking fire was doused, but smoldering. I heard Uncle's footsteps coming down the path. He still walked quickly, but his rhythm was off. It was Uncle's version of a limp. As soon as he was within sight, he started talking.

"I've ground enough corn, gathered enough wood and created enough defensible positions to last you the fourteen days I must be gone."

"Gone?"

"Yes. I must go."

"I'm worried to be alone again, Uncle. My legs aren't fully recovered."

"I told you, you must display utter loyalty! And loyalty means trust. I've made every arrangement so that the only walking you need to do outside of the yard in front of the Stone House is go down to the river and collect water. I've even fashioned a rope so you can drag multiple gourds on the trail. You may only go down to the river at high sun, and you must rub your body with the herbs from this pouch and cover yourself with this urine that I got from the cougar who attacked us."

"But, Uncle, I mean no disloyalty when I ask why you are leaving now. Is it possible for you to wait?"

"There is no waiting! I have no need to explain myself to you. Your very question is the height of disloyalty. Were you not already injured I would punish you now! The Mighty-One, praise his magnificence, may have you killed! I'm doing you no favors by letting this insolence slide, but I must maintain my energy for a speedy journey to the Crescent City. The only defense against the kind of attacks we saw is to appeal to the Mighty-One himself. I will also bring back another house girl. You need only concern yourself with maintaining your defenses against another attack. You must use everything you know. You must use fire, stone and Dreams. Your ultimate test of loyalty now, Redcloud, is to say safe and alive until I return. Have I made myself clear?" He adjusted the belt beneath his traveling cloak.

"Yes, Uncle. I will stay safe."

"And stay hidden! Especially at night."

"Yes, Uncle."

"I will call on you in Dreams, Redcloud, but you must not go near the ground where your Dreaming Hut once stood until I return. Do you understand?"

"Yes, Uncle."

With that, Uncle threw two water gourds across his back. His cloak flapped open in the breeze. His belt was laden with jerky. He marched down the same trail as he had before. Instead of seeming to float, he rolled. Above all, he was noisier, but he either didn't care or couldn't help but be conspicuous in his haste. As the uneven sound of his departure grew thinner in my ears, questions filled my mind. What happened to my protector? Was the Jaguar dead? As my legs were still in the process of healing, it seemed as though I would have a lot of time to think about them. I hoped these thoughts were not a sign of disloyalty.

## 10

# THE DREAM OF THE KING

The sun was already passed its zenith when I was roused from my sleep. The image of the Medicine Hut and the pouch in my mind almost caused my body to convulse. I thought about how to get there. Footprints would be difficult to hide in my condition. There was no way I could use a rope to climb over the patch of dirt as the House Girl had.

Then it occurred to me. Maybe I didn't have to walk or climb at all. Maybe I could Dream my way into the Medicine Hut as Uncle had Dreamed himself into flying me to the river. Uncle had never taught me the intricacies of such things. All of my instruction as a Dreamer, what little I remembered, was in how to make stars.

Deciding it was better to wait, I closed my eyes and attempted to rest. It was no use. As soon as I saw the back of my eyelids, the image assaulted me again. I knew in that the kind of Dream I was to have depended largely on my Will to have it as well as the song that I sang into the Dream. Would it be possible to use Uncle's So ng? Uncle never told me if songs only worked for one person over another. Even then, my memories usually failed me.

Closing my eyes again brought the Medicine Hut and the pouch I had seen in the House Girl's vision. I had to try something. I decided to sit as quietly and calmly as I could with my back against the wall. I closed my eyes, but this time, I didn't try to sleep. I merely sat awake with my eyes closed. In the blackness, other sensations became clearer. Once I started breathing, the image of the Medicine Hut interior immediately returned, but I wasn't asleep. I kept breathing steadily. I started to notice sounds in the background. I could hear birds calling. I heard stirring in the bushes. Squirrels, I thought. Even at my thought, the hut persisted.

I continued breathing as I heard the wind gathering momentum in the distance until a wave of wind passed by the Stone House. Then I heard nothing but my breath. Upon an exhale, a Song emerged. I continued singing until the image of the interior of the Medicine Hut became more than an image. It became something I could reach out and touch. I turned around to see the entrance flap of the hut closed with the harsh report of daylight behind. I Willed my other Dream Hand to open the flap.

At first, I took simple delight in the sensation that I could feel anything without using my own hands. Then it occurred to me that I might be leaving footprints, even in a Dream. I looked down to see my feet touching the floor of the hut. I lifted my foot to see the print beneath. As I looked at the footprint, my displeasure at the sight seemed to make it disappear, leaving the ground smooth. My delight caused my breathing to alter, and the image of the hut began to falter. I felt myself begin to fall, but I managed to resume my Song, and the hut resolidified. I reached my Dreaming

Hand toward the hidden spot where the House Girl's vision had told me I would find the pouch. I felt the weight of it as I pulled the pouch from its hidden perch.

The light showed my footprints. I Willed them to erase as before. Then it occurred to me that I probably wouldn't make footprints if I didn't allow my feet to feel the ground pressing against them. I felt the weight on my feet disappear slowly until it felt like I was floating on the dirt. When I lifted one foot out of the hut, there was no footprint left behind. It took all of my discipline to steady my enthusiasm! When I brought my other foot out from the hut, I dropped the flap and felt my Dreaming Body fall to the ground! First dust, then pouch, then blackness.

THE REPORT of night brought Uncle into my Dreams.

Utter loyalty! I thought. I heard Uncle's voice, but I saw only blackness.

"Rise! Rise up the ladder!"

In the jumping light of a fire shown through a doorway, I saw figures, children like me, coming up a ladder that was sticking out of a floor. As my Dreaming vision adjusted, the ladder looked more and more like the ladder I watched the House Girl go down before. This time, the children kept coming, one after the other. I'd never seen so many all at once. All of them wore cloth over their eyes. Each was guided along by placing their left hand on the shoulder of the person in front of them.

The House Girl emerged. She looked completely disoriented with the cloth covering her eyes. A young warrior standing to the side of the ladder guided her hand to the shoulder of the boy in front of her. He was shorter and skinnier than me. I felt a streak of envy as another boy, this one taller and more muscular, put his hand on her shoulder. I followed the House Girl in my Dreamer's vision. Should I have spoken to her? Would that have brought her comfort?

Even as I followed the House Girl, even as I began to see the curves of her face, the smoothness of her skin, I saw more and more children making an ever longer chain.

I followed as they were led into a large courtyard. Its walls only visible at the horizon as they obscured a small belt of stars that otherwise painted the night sky. I followed as the House Girl was arranged in a row of children that trailed off in the darkness in either direction. Even as my Dreamer's vision strained against the blackness of the new moon sky, I could tell that there was at least one row behind her and one row in front of her. There were no torches. I heard the sound of the fire in the room from which the House Girl emerged being doused along with several other fires elsewhere. There was no light to speak of except for the stars .

An adult voice began singing. It was Uncle. Another deeper and more resonant voice began singing with him. Slowly, all of the boys began joining the Song. More children became visible as the girls began swaying on their feet with the cloth still over their eyes. Then the girls began singing as well. Uncle's voice rose above them all, piercing the night sky. Drums sounded. Uncle and the other adults called out words in many languages. I heard one of the young warriors who surrounded the children shout, "See!" All the children removed the blindfolds from their eyes. All their eyes glowed like the stars, including those of the House Girl.

The singing became shrieking. Uncle's voice became that of a screaming eagle that cut through the rest. The drums stopped. He started another Song to which all the children responded by repeating phrases. The drums picked up the new pattern of Uncle's calls and the children's responses. Suddenly, Uncle began singing in my language, or was he putting these words in my head? I couldn't be sure, but I remember what the words were.

"We beseech you oh stars!
Revealers of secrets
Revealers of fortune.
Hear us now!
Move Heaven and Earth
Move Sun and Moon
Move secrets and fortune.
Move you mighty stars
Bend to the Will of your King!
The King of Kings!
The Chief of Chiefs
Who is mightier still
Than you!
Move oh stars!
Twist the hand of fate
Succumb to the Will of the Mightiest of the Mighty!
Submit!
Submit!
Submit!
Submit!"

All at once, the children raised their hands to the sky on a sustained note. The House Girl rose into the sky. Their eyes glowed ever brighter as they followed her.

I watched the House Girl turning majestically to face the night sky, but the stars did not move. She sang louder and louder with her compatriots. Her eyes grew brighter and brighter. Light emerged from her nose and throat as she began to spin, focusing a beam of light rising from the others. The light from the children's eyes revealed tears running down cheeks as their singing grew more desperate. Some began flailing their arms at the stars. The House Girl sang and spun with more intensity, but with none of the hysterics of the others. Her dignity caused my heart to race. My vision began to circle her to become absorbed into her as she sang with her spinning, waking body. Her other body, her Dreaming Body, smiled and motioned me into her Dreams.

THE SINGING STOPPED. It was daybreak, and we were alone. Her face glowed in the morning sun as though she had been waiting for this moment even longer than I had. A moment, a place where we could be alone. I reached out to touch her cheek. I felt my being tingle as she placed her hand on mine and closed her eyes in delight.

I have waited for you, she said in my mind. I have waited for you to become strong enough to Dream freely.

I have waited, too, I thought, but I don't remember waiting.

No, you can't remember things because the man you call your Uncle has been poisoning you.

But he has protected me! I've seen it!

He has protected you because he needs you.

How could he need me? He is a mighty warrior, and I am a bumbling child.

No, Redcloud. You're neither bumbling nor are you a child any longer, but you are blind. The man you call your Uncle has stolen your sight and your memories. I cannot give them back to you, but I can show you my memories.

Why aren't your memories stolen?

They were, but I found them when I stopped eating the corn he gave me.

Uncle has warned me of disloyalty. I have seen his anger and his power. His vision has brought me here. I am afraid to know your memories because I fear he may hurt you if he knows.

I know he brought you, her thoughts reverberated. I know he knows we are together now.

But why? Is he testing my loyalty?

I think he may be testing his own. You must know my memories, Redcloud. You must know them so you can restore your own memories. You are the only one who has that Power. I will show you that Power by sharing my memories with you.

At that moment, I fell into the brightness of her eyes. I saw a vast horizon of trees with the first rays of sunrise pushing shadow aside and giving red and gold and purple and blue back to the heavens. Sunrise had never been so majestic. My vision moved outside of my Will. I turned to see a fire with a pot suspended above it. It was fastened in a manner and with materials I had never seen before.

A young woman emerged from a straw hut just beyond the fire. It was the same young woman the House Girl had shown me before. She stood and smiled at me. I felt myself running toward her. I was impelled by an instinct that was as liberating as it was encompassing. I ran right into the woman's arms. I felt the warmth of her body as my arms grasped her about the waist. She ran her hands through my hair, her fingernails caressing my scalp. How could I have forgotten such joy? The sensation was so familiar. I ached for more, but the woman let go of me and, my arms fell to my side. She then took my cheeks into her hands and kissed me on the forehead and smiled. She spoke words of utter endearment in the language of the House Girl.

The man I had seen before also emerged from the hut behind the woman. He was tall and muscular as he wrapped an elk skin about his body and looked at the fire a moment. When he turned his eyes to me and the woman, he smiled so broadly I felt I might faint. I ran toward him and embraced him as well. His warmth was harder but no less welcoming. The smell of his strength gave me complete comfort. It was the first time I can remember such strength without any sense of menace or danger. My breath was deep and easy with these people.

These are my parents. The House Girl's thought penetrated the bliss. I always loved greeting them at dawn.

How did you remember this? I want to remember, too.

Not all memories are so pleasant.

I had the stinging sensation of rocks in my side and the smell of smoke and pine. I could see nothing, but I could hear fast, unsteady breathing. Again, the hand caressed my head. I heard screaming and burning in the background. A sliver of light revealed daylight reflecting off of yellow dirt. Somehow, I knew to keep still. There was a familiarity to this discomfort. I watched as the sliver of light slipped from daylight into moonlight. The breathing of the woman the House Girl called her mother had changed to the steady rhythm of sleep. My movement roused her. She let go of me only to cover my mouth in a gesture of implored silence. I let myself sit up. I watched as she slowly rose. The moonlight showed a mixture of sadness in her lips but hardened resolve in her eyes. She looked back at me and gestured for me to stay where I was. I felt myself nod. She slipped under the boughs of the squat pine tree where we had been hiding.

It was when she left my sight that the wind started blowing and I could smell the smoke again. It was not the smoke of wood alone, but the smoke of cloth and flesh. I felt nauseated as my guts began to convulse, but the heaves produced nothing as my stomach was empty.

I heard a scream from the other side of the tree. It was the House Girl's mother. I felt myself race around the tree to see the mother weeping over a body. It was hard to see in the moonlight, but the sight of her father's lifeless torso told me why her mother was crying .

The next memory found me walking through the piñon and juniper forest with the mother. She covered her head with the elk skin the father had used. There was no smile in her eyes. I felt the pinch of hunger in my stomach. The mother stopped in front of a piñon tree and began to rummage through the tree for pine cones that might contain nuts. There was a desperation to her movements. She pulled a cone, inspected it, smelled it, shook it, then threw it on the ground over her shoulder backward. I felt myself scramble to pick up the cone. I put it in my mouth, gnawing on it in an attempt to derive sustenance. There was nothing, but I gnawed further. The mother tossed another cone. Again, I gnawed. Again, nothing. Again, pinching.

Another image, another memory. More walking. The mother's face was gray, her cheeks hollow.

More cones, I tasted a nut. The flavor burst into my mouth.

Then I saw the mother lying on the path. She was breathing, but barely. I put my hand on her cheek as tears rolled down my face. As soon as my hand touched her cheek, another image stabbed my brain.

~

My belly stung as I saw a vision the House Girl had shown me before. Flames engulfed the horizon. There were shouts and screams. In the distance, I saw two enormous figures swinging clubs down on running bodies. They fell with screeches and thuds. Another swing, another blow, another body hit the ground. A sideways blow caused another body to leave the ground. A burst of flame revealed the face of one of the two enormous attackers. It was the face of the Mighty-One himself. As I felt my perspective shift, I saw the two bodies of the Mighty-One as ghastly skeletons mechanically hinging as firelight danced.

Utter loyalty! a thought shouted, but it was not the thought of the House Girl. It was the thought of Uncle. Had I lost her? Was this another memory, or was it a vision? Was it both? I saw Uncle picking me up and carrying me. His warmth was cold. His strength was frightening. His eyes brought no comfort.

This must have been one of Uncle's memories because I no longer saw the courtyard. I heard no songs. There was no spinning, celestial House Girl. It felt like I was rolling over in my sleep as the cold morning gave way to a warm, windy night. The only thing that was the same was the flickering, torch-lit shadow of the Mighty-One himself. As his single skeleton regained its flesh, his face was painted in a dark color or perhaps that was simply his color in all light. He stood wearing only a loincloth and two golden bracelets. His look was fierce.

Uncle's body was calm. He breathed evenly, but I could feel beads of sweat gathering beneath his tunic.

"What news from the Star-Talkers, my pet?"

"Oh, Lord! The news is not favorable."

"Not favorable?" The Mighty-One walked forward revealing his massive hands. "Not favorable," he repeated.

"Hmm. I sense no disloyalty in such an outrage. You would test your life by telling me something unfavorable?"

"I must, Highness. If I were to keep this news from you, it would be the height of disloyalty."

"Ah! You may be spared my wrath at this unfavorable news. You and you alone."

"Your Mightiness is most merciful."

"Proceed, Shapeshifter."

"Yes, Highness. The Star-Talkers have been given a new prophecy. This prophecy states that your reign must end in this world when the stars show as bright as day."

"Treachery!" The Mighty-One lunged toward Uncle.

"Please, Highness, know that my sharing this with you is only in the interest of my loyalty to you! I beg Your Mightiness' mercy for my devotion. There is a way through this prophecy where Your Greatness can grow beyond all measure."

"There is nothing greater than my rule, Shapeshifter! You bore witness to the chaos and confusion that ruled this land before my era of plenty!"

"Of course, Your Highness, the land was ravaged with plague and backward vision."

"It was I who raised these buildings. It was I who paid homage to the gods of old by providing them with leadership and guidance! It was I who captured the Sun itself in our windows! How then can the stars speak such blasphemy!? My reign! My reign is absolute! It is beyond perfection. The people thrive at my whim!"

"Of course, Majesty!"

"These Star-Talkers of yours. They have lost their vision. Not only have their eyes burnt out of daylight, but they have burnt out of night as well. You must start again,

Shapeshifter. Yes! They have lost their vision. You must start again, or you shall lose yours!"

"But Highness ..."

"Do not interrupt me!" The wind gave report of the blow that would knock Uncle to the ground several paces from where he was standing. "Your pack of Star-Talkers has outlasted itself! They must be purged."

Uncle pulled himself back to his feet. "If that is the will of Your Majesty, then, of course, it shall be done, but there is a warning in this prophecy that I must make clear to your Mightiness out of my devotion to Your Greatness. I humbly beseech Your Highness to hear this warning."

The Giant spun on his heel and faced away from Uncle as he gathered his composure. The muscles in his legs rippling like a raging river . He spoke with his back turned to Uncle. "Proceed."

"Highness, the prophecy gives no detail as to when this calamity will take place. Its reference to the stars showing as bright as day has no correspondence to what we know of the stars in their march across the sky. At this time, I don't know what it means. If you eliminate our Star-Talkers altogether, you run the risk of never learning anything more as Star-Talking can only be done by those hidden from the daylight. If you allow them to die in their own time, according to tradition, you may learn more about how to eliminate this outrage instead of just the Star-Talkers themselves."

"No, they must die now. They have seen blasphemy!"

"Please, if Your Highness will permit me."

The Giant turned again upon his heel to face Uncle. This time more slowly. As he steadied himself, another Giant, a twin or a double, stepped to the side of his original body. The double's eyes glowed with white coals.

"You were saying?" they asked in unison.

Uncle bowed at this show of strength. "If it is Your will, these blasphemers will be slaughtered straight away, but I would beg Your Mightiness to train a new breed of Star-Talkers. A breed apart from these flawed creatures. A breed that not only talks to the stars but can order them to do Your Majesty's will! Let this new breed be an extension of Your Highness' power instead of a witness to blasphemy!"

"You have my permission to proceed, Shapeshifter. You will give me the means to gain ultimate power over the stars themselves, but first, these blasphemers are to be slaughtered, the blasphemers themselves and all of those who gave rise to them. The people must know my wrath!"

"Of course, Highness. I will train this new breed of Star-Talkers from the ashes of Your Majesty's revenge." Uncle bowed.

"To ruin!" With that shout, both the Giant and his double took an ax and a club in either hand and went down into the rooms where the Star-Talkers spent their days in total blackness. I felt Uncle refocus his disgust at the innocent screams being snuffed out by the Giant as he slashed and beat them to death below. Uncle had to refocus his disgust on blasphemy itself, or he knew his head would also be shattered. Uncle even managed a twinge of admiration. At least he has the courage to face the horror of his decisions himself.

This was the first time Uncle had ever allowed me to hear his thoughts when they weren't addressed to me. Most of his thoughts to me were commands. This thought revealed even more of his stubborn brilliance. His instinct to survive in the face of overwhelming power.

## 11

## THE BINDING & THE BLINDING

More memories flashed. Each more horrid than the last. I was beginning to lose track of where I was, of who I was, of when I was. Was I still Dreaming in the Stone House? Was I still witnessing the memories of the House Girl? Was Uncle still directing my consciousness? Would I ever be able to direct it on my own?

The vision of my mind settled back on Uncle as he accompanied the Giant on many of his missions of revenge. The Giant would go about in a blind rage burning and smashing all that he saw, but Uncle was more selective. Uncle singled out and protected children. While he never directly contradicted the Giant, Uncle would enter a village in the shape of a crow or a squirrel or some other creature of little note. After locating children, he would shift his gaze. His vision would become blurred for a time, then all of the world would begin to glow in a sun-like fashion, in slivers of light flowing like the fur of an animal in a breeze. It was the same kind of quality that Uncle shimmered with when I gazed upon him during my rescue from the cougars. Each child had a distinctive pattern of countless strings of light.

Indeed, sometimes Uncle's vision would blur to the degree that each child shone with the same quality as the sun itself. It was dazzling to behold.

~

LOURDES COULDN'T HELP but ask, *Is this Seeing, Redcloud?*

*Yes this is Seeing, but this Seeing happened because I was experiencing Uncle's memories, not because I had learned to do it on my own. I will explain soon, but the others are watching! Please stay hidden for now.*

*Are the others the Cougars from before?*

*Of a sort, I can't explain now. Please trust me and let me continue!*

~

MY ASTONISHMENT sometimes caused my concentration to falter only to hear Uncle's thought, *Loyalty!* pounding me back into focus.

After he found the particular children he was looking for, he turned himself into a cougar. It pained me to watch as he mauled innocent people in their sleep in order to drive their children into the forest, only to be corralled by the armies of the Giant. Uncle had a particular interest in babies, although his pattern of theft showed that he also needed some older children. The last memory broke the bond of my consciousness with Uncle.

In this memory, he entered a village of low-slung huts. There were no crops or fields to speak of. These people lived by hunting and foraging alone. As a crow, Uncle spotted a young girl. My heart leaped at her familiar nature. She was already separated from her family. Uncle began a series of dives to separate her further. As the House Girl began to scream, her parents emerged from a hut. In the middle-distance, fires had already been set. The Giant and his double had already begun the slaughter. The House Girl's father ran off with his club as the Girl and her mother dove underneath the protection of the boughs of a squat pine tree with its thin, green needles. The tree began to glow not with fire but with energy. An energy with an intensity that could burn the skin off of those who looked at it directly.

My consciousness began to tumble again. Rolling, spinning, grasping. Where was my body? I found myself back in the courtyard of the Crescent City. The children were still swaying and singing in the moonless night. The House Girl continued spinning above them. Uncle, his face creased with age, leading them in their chants.

I felt my own body heave again. *I must return to my wounds. I must be direct. My return must be one of complete and utter loyalty!*

MY BODY NEEDED ME, but I couldn't find it. I tried to feel my fingers, but were they my fingers? Were they hers? Were they his? I tried to feel my breath. Was I dead?

The Dreams of star-making were so distinct, that world so different, finding my way home simply meant going back to comfort. Now, there was no comfort. There was no difference. There was only dread. *Let me then, at least, find love.* Then I was back to the courtyard, back to the House Girl spinning, back to blackness. The singing had grown in intensity. The notes had gone beyond language. The House Girl had merged herself with the consciousness of all of those singing. Still all of them reached through the House Girl. All of them reached out just as I had learned to reach out to my prey. They reached across time and space. They reached into the Heavens themselves!

I had to let go, or was I pushed away? My perspective became that of Uncle's. While this familiarity brought little comfort, I was no longer being stretched to infinity. No, Uncle wasn't stretching. Uncle was squeezing. Uncle was connected to yet others. These others hemmed in the stars even as the Star-Talkers begged them to move. He felt like rocks at the bank of a river. He was singing one Song to the courtyard, the Song of Reaching, but his other, his double, was singing the Song of Collapse and guiding. One Song was ecstatic, the other was maniacally controlled. Again, I felt myself being ripped apart. Then, it happened.

The sky went from mysterious blackness nesting small pools of light to an inferno of light. Was this sunrise? I felt Uncle's eyes begin to burn, or were they the House Girl's? Then I felt something else. It was not burning. It was stinging. I felt my legs again! My breath heaved. Upon a triumphant inhale, I opened my own eyes, but I could hardly believe them. The crickets gave word of night, but a strange, powerful light shone underneath the elk-skin door to the Stone House. My tongue was rough against the roof of my mouth. My dressings were dry. I took a water gourd and drank liberally. Then I carefully slid on my backside toward the door.

I lay down and poked my head out underneath the elk-skin door. The sky was an unnatural color, a strange hue of purple and gold, a perpetual twilight. It strains my expression to describe it, but either the sun had gotten smaller, or there was a new sun.

I heard the hoot of an owl that landed on the ground, disoriented. The growl of a gigantic throat roused the owl's attention as well as my own. Two enormous glowing eyes swayed into the clearing in front of the Stone House. The owl managed to fly out of sight as the Jaguar arrived. I froze. The mighty cat walked with slow dignity toward the Stone House, toward me. My breathing became deep, almost serene. Another rolling hum came from inside the Jaguar, a greeting? It walked closer to the house and bowed its massive head. It started sniffing. Another low growl, then it licked its nose. A sudden grunt through its nose brought a strange comfort to me. A few more steps brought the cat's head right above mine as I lay across the threshold of the Stone House. It then sat on its haunches and surveyed the strangeness. Another grunt brought it to a lying position. My head tilted into the ground to reveal its giant upside-down nose barely an arm's length from my head.

I didn't realize how wide open my eyes were until the Jaguar closed its own in what felt like an act of affection. Clearly, if it had meant me harm, I would have been dead. I felt a smile cross my face. It seemed the cat smiled as well.

I slid back into the Stone House and drank some more water. Against my better judgment, I ate some jerky. Another rush of breath reminded me of my new companion. I took a piece of jerky, moved the elk skin aside and tossed it out the door.

"Thank you," I said aloud. These were the first words I had spoken in days.

THE DAY REMAINED DAY, and I began to miss the night. Even as the old sun set, the new sun remained. The Jaguar stood vigil outside the doorway of the Stone House. I changed my dressings. I was surprised to see how gruesome the wounds were and how quickly they had healed. I experimented with getting on all fours as my knees were not wounded. Finding some confidence, I used the wall of the Stone House to lift myself to one foot. I winced at lifting my leg, but momentum dictated that I continue. Upon standing, my pain lessened, but anytime I had to steady myself, the stabbing persisted. I was in no condition to walk. I looked around the room, forlorn.

Now I would have to go back to the ground without using my thighs. Slow didn't seem best, so I decided to fall as gracefully as possible. I tried to land on my backside but missed and landed on my hip. Thankfully, the dirt was softer than I thought it would be but painful, nonetheless. I managed to scoot myself back to the sleeping mat and catch my breath. It would be days before I could go anywhere with my own body.

I drank some more water. I managed to relieve myself out the front door while lying on my side. I don't know why I thought so, but the Jaguar seemed to approve.

As soon as I lay back down, I was seized once again by a Dream. A cascade of images flowed through me. An explosion of light, and the burning of all the eyes of the courtyard. I saw rows of children roughly my age keeled over in agony. My perspective fell quickly on the House Girl. No longer spinning above the rest, she sat with her knees to her chest and her eyes closed. Tears streamed down her face. The others sitting next to her seemed far worse off. They wailed, kicking and screaming. Their hands clasping their eyes, crying tears of blood.

"Did the stars move?" the Giant's voice thundered over the wails.

"I can't tell, Highness. There is a new star in the sky. It has blocked out all the others. It looks to have blinded many of the Star-Talkers."

"Has this changed the prophecy? Have these dregs we've stolen wasted themselves already?"

"Perhaps, Mighty-One. The only thing I know for certain is that we must Dream on this, you and I."

"You are my Dreamer, Shapeshifter."

"We will Dream together."

"They have failed me! They were not loyal enough! The Star-Talkers must die!"

"Highness, it would take many seasons to train new Star-Talkers. So many are already blinded, but they do not need their eyes to talk to the stars."

"No, but they have their mouths and ears to talk to each other! They must pay for this outrage!"

"Of course, they must, Mighty-One, but patience may be the order of the day. Let us consult with the Sun Daggers. Perhaps your father, the Sun, and your mother, the Moon, can give you understanding of these events. Maybe they can tell us directly that the prophecy has been changed. Maybe then, we can have further use for these Star-Talkers. Perhaps they can make your Power even greater. The new star might be an omen of even greater triumphs to come for Your Mightiness."

"Greater triumphs? Can there be a greater triumph than ruling all I survey?"

"Perhaps this new star can shed light on even more worlds for Your Mightiness to conquer. Your parents can tell you. The Daggers will know."

"Greater triumph. Yes. The Daggers will know!"

"If it pleases Your Mightiness, I shall return to my house in the country to retrieve the medicine necessary for the journey to the Sun Daggers."

"I need no medicine, Shapeshifter. I am invincible!"

"Of course, Your Mightiness, the medicine is for me, so

that I may interpret the Will of your father and mother when we return to the Daggers."

"Your weakness is nauseating to me."

"Mighty-One, I submit to your will. If my frailty is offensive to Your Greatness, you have but to snap your fingers to crush me into oblivion."

"Why do you state the obvious?"

"A thousand pardons, Mightiness. The medicine will also be used to minister to the Star-Talkers in case they turn out to remain useful." Uncle kneeled prostrate before the Giant.

The Giant looked out over his courtyard. The wailing had changed to sobs. "Kill every fourth!" he shouted. "Put the rest back in their holes. And bring four for me, including that disaster of a spinner!"

*Undying loyalty!* Uncle thought, but I couldn't tell if it was for me, the Giant or both of us until I saw who the Giant meant by the "spinner." The House Girl had ceased weeping when she was brought before the Giant. While the three others quivered and sobbed, she stood erect. She comported herself as only a warrior could when her skull was cracked open by the Giant's club.

*All loyalty!* Uncle's thoughts scratched in my mind.

MY THIGHS WERE STINGING as I shouted in disbelief. I was sitting up, my vision blurred with tears. The Jaguar roared and paced just outside the door. The shock of the sound sent terror through my grief. The report of another high-pitched growl meant the Cougar had returned. The Jaguar roared a thousand drums in return. There was the sound of branches breaking as the Cougar apparently escaped. The

Jaguar roared again. The trees rustled. Then, all was silent. I heard the Jaguar resume its perch next to the door.

What was I to do? Uncle was returning in as many as ten days. Nothing was the same. How could I swear loyalty to the butcher who murdered my love? I needed the House Girl's pouch, now more than ever. I would have no choice but to use my Dreaming Body to retrieve it. This would be a true test of the Jaguar's loyalty to me. Was he Uncle's protector or mine? If the Jaguar was Uncle's spy and saw my Dreaming Body with the pouch, then I was undone. Even if the Jaguar remained loyal to my physical body, would it allow my Dreaming Body to pass unharmed? If the Jaguar attacked my Dreaming Body, would it harm my physical body? There could be no answers without action.

## 12

# THE RESCUE OF THE POUCH

I must have fallen asleep as the next thing I remember was bird song. The harsh light under the elk-skin door betrayed day.

In order to carry out the House Girl's final wish, I had to take hope that Uncle would not have the strength to watch me while he was actually walking. All of my activities with regard to the Medicine Hut had to be done during the day. I would have to take great care never to reveal them in my Dreams at night when Uncle was more likely to visit. My very survival might rest upon my success. If I was able to move the pouch with my Dreaming Body, then perhaps I could bring more water as well. I was down to my last four gourds, not enough water to last until Uncle returned. The steady breathing of the Jaguar raised another obstacle, but no time could be lost to doubt.

I did my best to shade the two windows as well as the door. I lay down on my mat and I began to sing the same Song as before. As I drew breath for each new phrase of the Song, I fell deeper and deeper into the blackness of my physical body until a sliver of light appeared in the notes of the Song. That sliver grew more and more brilliant as my perspective fell toward it. Then, I felt another breath.

The second breath started out synchronous with the breath in my physical body but grew in strength. My Song became the wind in the ears of my Dreaming Body.

My Dreaming Body stood outside Uncle's Medicine Hut. I performed the maneuver of lifting my feet from the dirt so as not to leave my footprints. I then began to walk in small steps, recalling the fall from before. I heard the low grumble of the Jaguar at the doorway of the Stone House. Hearing it from two different directions began to break my concentration, but I forced myself back to the rhythm of breathing established in the Song. Once again, another step and another until I reached the deer-hide flap of the hut, as it lay open in the wind. The pouch was lying at the threshold.

I felt my hand reaching for it on the ground. I found myself trying to steady my body as I reached. When my hand was upon the pouch, it passed right through it.

The shock of frustration caused my breath to heave in both bodies as the pouch leaped into the air over the head of my Dreaming Body and landed just behind it. I began to laugh. The unsteady breathing caused my Dreaming Body to move erratically. I spun around to watch the pouch dancing on the path to the rhythm of my laughter. Once again, the gentle grunt from the Jaguar re-centered my concentration. While my movement did not produce any footprints, the dance of the pouch had left marks in the dirt. I also had to contend with closing the hut in a way so that Uncle would never suspect I had been there.

Two things crossed my mind as I consciously maintained a steady breath to keep my body where it was. First, why had the hands of my Dreaming Body functioned so effortlessly before when I dropped the pouch in the first place? Second, why didn't I need to use my hands to erase my footprints before? I was sure these were questions Uncle could answer, but I certainly couldn't ask him. Whatever Uncle's designs, he didn't seem to want me exploring my Dreams on my own. It must have terrified him to leave me alone. *Strange,* I thought, *Uncle could be afraid not only for his own life but also for mine? Why?*

Another breath cleared my mind. Somehow, thinking about Uncle too much didn't seem wise.

My Dreaming Body seemed to function in the real world similarly to the way it functioned in my Dreams of star-making. It was not hands that made things move or happen but thought itself, a special kind of thought, Willful thought, insistence. With that, I insisted that the flap of the hut be closed. Instantly, the flap of the hut was where I envisioned it. It didn't even appear to move.

Then I realized I had to fix the markings of the pouch on the threshold. The flap of the hut disappeared in the same manner as before. My perspective of the threshold became as though I were sniffing the ground like an animal. The dirt became smooth. Then it became smoother still, then yet smoother until it had the consistency of the standing water in a puddle. *Wait! Wait!*

I felt my body burst into the air, then fall back to earth . I managed to stop myself before I hit the ground. Once again, steadying my breath to keep my body above the earth so as not to disturb the dirt below. My physical body heard the Jaguar grunt with more urgency, perhaps lifting its head. Had it seen my leap?

Resuming song breath, I came back to my Dreaming Body's senses. I had only leaped a few paces from the entrance of the hut. The door was still wide open, and the dirt was still as smooth as water. As I looked at the patterns of the surrounding dirt, I envisioned the dirt in the threshold in the same pattern and it changed instantly, but that too seemed out of place. Then I looked at the pattern of the dirt on the path to the hut.

*Yes*, I thought, and another breath rearranged the pattern in a vision more appropriate. Still another breath closed the flap of the hut. I then looked at the pouch and breathed a vision of it in the hand of my Dreaming Body. It leaped to my hand in obedience. My hands now seemed to possess solidity.

Now I had the pouch. It was time to find out how perceptive my guardian was.

I LOOKED toward where the ring of shrubs that surrounded the Medicine Hut met the small path to the Stone House. Instead of taking the small steps as I had done before, would it be possible to insist my Dreaming Body to the ring of shrubs? It was only four or five paces. Still, it seemed better to move more slowly with the pouch in my hands. I began taking the small steps as before. When I reached the ring of trees, I turned around. I saw no evidence of footprints, and the door to the hut was just as I remembered it when I first arrived. As gently as possible, I insisted the branches be moved aside, and my Dreaming Body stepped out onto the path that I had used to build the barrier earlier. It had many sets of footprints. I arranged my Dreaming Body so that its footprints would be in alignment with the others. This allowed the body to feel its own weight and sink into the dirt. After that, I could walk in the same manner as my physical body. As I did this, the pouch began to take on a new weight. Whatever the House Girl had packed inside, it was very dense.

I slowed down as I rounded the path to come to the clearing with the Stone House. The Jaguar grunted in a familiar fashion. This was the first time I'd ever seen it during the day. Its body was propped up against the side of the house. As I came into view, it picked up its head and licked its nose. I took another step. The Jaguar stood up slowly and licked its nose again. Was it hungry? Undoubtedly. I was only able to feed it some of my jerky, of which I saw at least two pieces lying in the clearing between the door and the fireplace. Perhaps it knew the jerky was tainted?

The Jaguar began walking slowly toward my second body. I felt my breath go deeper into my abdomen. Was my physical body breathing more deeply, or was it my Dreaming Body? *Keep the rhythm of the Song!* I thought.

As the Jaguar approached, my breath was finding deeper and deeper reserves. *Steady!* I could hear the Jaguar sniffing the air in my Dreaming Body's direction. Could it smell my fear? If there was anything to smell, it would definitely be fear.

*Steady!*

The cat stopped just one or two paces in front of me and extended its nose toward the pouch. It sniffed again while gently closing its eyes. It then walked past me as it gently rubbed its great head against my Dreaming Body. My breath dropped lower still. My perception changed. I saw flickers of light that looked like shooting stars, but they were coming up from the ground.

*Steady!*

*Walk slowly*, said another thought. It was neither my own nor was it Uncle's. It wasn't the House Girl's either. I turned my head to see the Jaguar look at me again; it closed its eyes gently.

*Are those your thoughts?*

The Jaguar nodded. *It is not easy for me to communicate in your thoughts, but yes. You are safe for now. The herbs you possess will heal you in one way but expose old scars in another. Keep your breathing steady. I must eat.*

*Who are you?*

*There are no explanations for you now, only healing. I shall return. You may Dream of yourself only in this clearing.*

The Jaguar walked to the edge of the clearing and urinated on a large tree. My Dreaming Body walked toward the entrance to the Stone House. Both bodies heard the Jaguar's footsteps. I insisted the flap to the house open. I heard the whoosh of the flap from both my physical body as well as my Dreaming Body. Another two steps and my Dreaming Body saw my physical body sleeping.

My breath heaved. I heard the pouch drop to the floor of the Stone House and sight returned to my physical body. I looked over and reached for the pouch. It was even heavier than it had felt before. I carefully unfastened the flap. A new aroma emerged, both pleasant and powerful. I felt an instant sense of relief in my legs but an instant sense of fear in my heart.

I dipped my finger into the powder in the pouch. It tingled on the end of my finger. I placed a tiny amount on the end of my tongue, and a flash of lightning passed through me. My breath heaved once more. A few more breaths brought me back to focus. *Uncle can never know I have this,* I thought, *but where to hide it? How?*

I fastened the pouch closed and reasoned that I could use the powder to make tea, but I couldn't use any of the dishes Uncle would be familiar with. While a smoldering cooking fire would be expected, new dishes or this powder's smell on old ones would be suspicious. Uncle was perceptive in ways I couldn't understand. A rising fear grew as I realized I would have to establish a new camp away from here. It would need to be hidden from Uncle, so it would have to be built during the day in a place Uncle would never think to look. I would have to take great precautions to keep my memories of this place out of my Dreams at night. And what of the pouch? The Jaguar had already seen it, already smelled it. It told me I couldn't leave the clearing of the Stone House with my Dreaming Body.

Maybe there was a way to shield my memories from my Dreaming Body? According to the House Girl, Uncle had already shielded my own memories from my own consciousness, perhaps if my Dreaming Body ate some of Uncle's cornmeal, it would forget about the pouch and Medicine Hut. That would mean construction of this new camp would have to take place with my physical body. Still another problem, I would have to hide this pouch long before another camp could be constructed. The longer I kept it in the Stone House, the more the scent would linger.

I set the pouch on the floor and licked the remaining powder from my fingers until the last remnants of its brownish color disappeared from view. Once again, my body felt a surge of energy. I spun around on all fours. Then slowly, I stood. My thighs still tingled, but there was no longer a stabbing pain. I bent down to pick up the pouch and walked outside. My eyes adjusted to the late afternoon sunlight. The Jaguar said I should only Dream within the compound, but it never said I couldn't walk elsewhere. Still, the Cougar would probably come after me if it found me. I went back inside and picked up one of Uncle's clubs. There could be no fault in defending myself, could there?

13

# THE DRAGGING

The late hour made it unlikely that I would be able to find a suitable site to begin my work, but I could take a walk to loosen my legs, and I needed water.

Marveling at the strength of the House Girl's powder, I stepped out into the compound. I felt the weight of Uncle's club. I didn't remember ever having used it before. I tried to remember how he placed his feet on the ground when he swung it in his attempt to kill the Cougar when I was mauled. I spread my feet out as I remembered. I raised the club with my dominant hand and swung it. The whoosh of the swing inspired my confidence. I swung it a few more times, alternating which side of my body the club whooshed. Each swing made my legs tingle with a new stretch. Old muscles, long forgotten, reporting for duty. I stepped forward with a swing at an imaginary enemy. I had to recover my balance from the momentum of the swing. I stepped back with yet more muscles coming alive, around my hips and backside. I tried one more time. This time, the balance was better, but the swing had less power. I was certainly not ready to do battle with a raging cougar, but Uncle was moving closer by the minute.

Uncle was as wise as he was ruthless. I decided that I would have to adopt the same kind of loyalty toward him that he directed me to feel toward the Mighty-One. The very notion stabbed my heart as the image of the Giant's club swinging toward the House Girl rushed into my thoughts. A breath, another, more controlled breath, a third, deeper. Calm.

As I looked at the rope with eight empty gourds attached lying against the house, loyalty toward Uncle was not so hard to feel. As far as I knew, he was the only person who had ever cared for me at all except for The ... Her ...

*With everything I do to protect myself, I can be of better service to my Uncle and the Mighty-One*, I thought. *Loyalty and service!* I was finding a spot for the new Dreaming Hut to spare Uncle the anguish of fear for my safety.

With that, I took up the rope with the empty gourds and marched, at least that's how I thought of it, down to the riverbank, club at the ready.

I made such a racket. I was sure the Cougar, the Jaguar and every other creature in the forest knew where I was. As I walked, I saw the Jaguar's footprints in the dirt. It must have been terribly thirsty. I scanned the foliage on either side of the path. While the grass made excellent cover for rabbits, it wouldn't suffice for my new hut. Uncle missed very little under his nose.

As I came under the airy shadow of the cottonwood trees at the river's edge, my legs felt better. This thought came as a relief when I realized I would have to drag the eight gourds attached to my rope filled with water up the hill to the Stone House. My journey back would not be so easy.

As the path widened into the clearing, I looked for any sign of the Cougar, but none was evident. The Jaguar's footprints went straight to the edge of the water and disappeared into the transparent pool I would use to fill the gourds. The Jaguar must have gone into the river itself as I didn't see another set of footprints leading away from the riverbank. My protector could swim. Beyond the pool, the brown water moving by in its silent momentum made me think of how brave and strong the Jaguar must be.

I looked across to the opposite bank as I began filling the gourds. If I could swim, the other side of the river would be an ideal place to hide my new Dreaming Hut. I had never tried to swim and didn't remember Uncle ever teaching me. I wasn't even sure if Uncle knew himself. *All the better for his protection,* I thought in a burst of loyalty. Still, drowning hardly seemed an act of loyalty. I lifted the gourd out of the river and sealed it off. As I attached the knot to the longer rope, I thought, *This weight, times eight.*

I scanned the other bank.

*So perfect, so loyal*, I thought. *So simple, yet so difficult.*

I roped off the second gourd and fastened it to the larger rope. Then I started filling gourd number three. I looked down the length of the river in the direction the water flowed, east, away from the sun as it started to set. At gourd number four, my fatigue at this task was beginning to show itself. As number five bubbled away underwater and became heavier, I looked down the river toward the sunset. There was no obvious way to cross without swimming in either direction. Perhaps I could do it with my Dreaming Body. *No,* I thought. *I can barely lift a pouch. How am I going to leap over this mighty river?*

Gourd number six, filled and fastened. Gourd number seven. Perhaps the Jaguar could help me. If it were to betray me to Uncle, even accidentally, I would be punished, but I would be acting out of loyalty. Gourd number seven, heavy. Gourd number eight, heavier. All fastened to the larger rope.

*Now the real work begins.*

THE EFFORT TO drag the gourds to the clearing in front of the house was successful but exhausting. I was hungry and thirsty. The sun was red on the horizon when I heard a rumble from the path to the west. I picked up Uncle's club. I heard footsteps as the Jaguar came into view. Relief and awe overcame me as I put down the club, and the cat resumed its perch next to the door.

I started a fire from embers and cooked some of Uncle's cornmeal. I decided to take the chance of adding a pinch of the herbs from the pouch. While there was no way to be sure, the hope was that this powder would somehow counteract Uncle's herbs. Something inside me felt that this idea was a bit foolhardy, but this thought occurred to me after I had already added the powder.

*I trust you, Uncle,* I thought for good measure.

I was beginning to learn how to separate streams of thought. Now that my memories were staying with me, I could begin to feel the difference between a memory and thought in one stream, and a memory and a thought in another. Uncle must have learned this, too. He was able to hide not only my own memories from me, but his memories as well. I wondered if his admonitions of loyalty toward the Mighty-One had masked another stream. This gave rise to another notion. I needed to be cautious in how I expressed my loyalty to Uncle. His avarice for loyalty was not so desperate as the Mighty-One's. The renaming helped blot away the terror of memory ...

The House Girl, a blast of feelings, images, and pictures came upon me. Uncle had never told me he saw the House Girl's visions. Uncle could not see pictures! ... At least not the pictures in my mind. He could definitely hear thoughts as words but not see pictures, at least not those of the House Girl. Thus, whatever must be hidden from Uncle must be construed only in pictures, not words. His loyalty must be words. Words, not of fear, but of affection.

As I ate the cornmeal, my consciousness continued in this vein of strategy. In the work of Dreams, strategic consciousness seemed to be the only way to survive.

## 14

# THE CROSSING

The gentle breathing of the cat swayed me to sleep. This sleep was sounder than any I could recall. There were no Dreams, save one.

*Redcloud!* Uncle called.

*Yes, Uncle?*

*I journey toward you in all loyalty to the Mighty-One. You must look to your defenses as I make my way home. Please find a small pouch of herbs under the blanket on my cot and add them to your morning tea. No doubt, you will be running out of water soon. These herbs will give you temporary strength as you recover, so you can refill your gourds. Drink liberally at the river and urinate as much as possible down the path to the river as well as around the Stone House and my Medicine Hut. Go back to the river and fetch more water to complete this task if you must.*

*In addition to temporary strength, these herbs will change the smell of your urine to frighten off the Cougar until I return. I'm sure the markings I left have faded. After you do this, you must continue to rest as we have much to accomplish upon my return and very little time in which to accomplish it,* he thought.

*Yes, Uncle, I recover slowly, but I will do as you ask.*

*All loyalty!*

*All loyalty!*

Uncle's thoughts that night were strident but tired. Upon the end of our communication, I fell into the blackness of total sleep. Joyful, total sleep!

THE SUN WAS ALREADY past the horizon when I woke. The joy of sitting up without pain made me smile. The Jaguar seemed to grunt in approval outside at his perch near the door to the Stone House. Uncle would likely keep traveling until dusk, which meant I had the day to do what he asked of me as well as do what I must for myself.

I retrieved the pouch per Uncle's instructions. It was tightly wrapped to conceal its odor, which was strong. Stronger even than the pouch left by the House Girl. I moved about to all four corners of the room. Then I made an offering to the six directions by waving the pouch for good measure. As I finished swinging the loosely closed pouch toward the ground, I heard the Jaguar sneeze.

*Disgusting!* The thought reverberated in my mind.

*Is that you, my Protector?*

*Would your old man think as much?*

*He is my Uncle, and I am loyal to him.*

*Loyal though you may be, he is no kin of yours. Your scents do not match as kin! The scent you just released is making me ill!*

*My apologies, Protector!*

I closed the pouch immediately. *I must continue my apologies, Protector, as my Uncle instructed me to use it to keep the Cougar you chased off earlier at bay.*

*It is effective in the short term. This monstrous scent is what kept me away from you for the two days after your old man left you injured.*

*I must follow his instructions and spread the scent to prove I remain loyal.*

*If that must be, then I must leave you for at least another two days.*

I stepped outside of the Stone House after placing the pouch on the cot where I found it.

Upon seeing me, the Jaguar raised his massive head to greet me.

*I can delay spreading the scent for a day, but if it's possible, I need your help until Uncle returns.*

*What do you need from me?*

*I need you to carry me across the great river.*

*What makes you think I can do that?*

*Are you able to cross it?* I asked.

*Of course! I keep my meals over on the other side so as to distract unwelcome visitors. An old habit I picked up when I was young.*

*Most wise!*

*Perhaps, but I have never carried anything across such an expanse of water. Do you swim, young one?*

*No. I have never learned.*

*Ah, yes, learning. I remember it fondly. My life as what I am means learning has been increasingly less necessary until very recently. Until I was sent to you.*

*You were sent to me? By whom?*

*I'm not sure. My thoughts are not clear enough to communicate such a thing, but I can say this. If you're prepared to risk your life crossing that river, then I'm prepared to help you. However, you'll need to drink some of the herbs from the first pouch you showed me,* he thought as his eyes blinked. *They are far less noxious and they seem to give you strength.*

*Yes, we'll both need strength as I will need to cross and return tomorrow.*

*Twice in one day!*

*I need to build a structure there, and I need to be back here so my Uncle will find me where he expects me.*

*Hiding something from your old man, are you?*

*I choose to call it a gift. A gift that will ensure our good graces to the Mighty-One who protects us all!*

*Ha! Ha! Ha!* the Jaguar roared with glee. *You have strength young one!*

I quickly unburied the herbs the House Girl had left for me and made some tea. I took care to set aside my dishes too, so I could use them the next day with Uncle's herbs and complete my instructions from him. By midmorning, the Jaguar and I were at the bank of the river. Its serenity became more and more menacing.

*Relax, young one! You're breathing like prey. Most unbecoming. I will share with you the two things you must know about swimming.*

*That would be much appreciated, Protector!*

*The first thing is to kick like a fish swims. Step up to the water and look at the way the fish swim in the pool where you filled your gourds. See how they flip their tails?*

*They look as though they are walking through the water.*

*Running boy! Running at the trunk and flipping at the claws!*

*You mean flip my toes?*

*Yes! Toes! See how the water glides past their whole body? Show me!*

I kicked my foot out from the thigh.

*Yes! Now flip the end of your foot!*

I attempted another kick from my thigh, but flipping my foot caused my sandal to fly into the bushes.

*That's the way, but you're going to have to get rid of those false feet!*

*But I need them if I am to walk long distances,* I thought as I went to retrieve the flying sandal.

*Sounds like you'll have to attach them to your rope in the same manner that you attach your water gourd.*

As I attached my sandals to the rope, I thought, *What's the second thing I need to know?*

*Ah, yes! You must move as though you had already reached land on the other side until there is no water, only land!*

With that, the Jaguar took one end of a gourd rope in its mighty jaws, and I took the other end.

*Onward to the other side!* he thought.

"Onward!" I shouted, thrilled to hear my own voice.

He lunged forward, and I held tight to the rope kicking my feet as he had told me to do. I promptly took in a mouthful of water and began to choke. The cat circled around me.

*Turn over on your back and keep your face above the water!* his thoughts shouted. *Spit the water out of your mouth!*

I heard his thoughts, but I went back under. Then I felt his enormous strength lifting me to the surface.

*Cough it out! Keep your face toward the sky and your legs outstretched and straight.*

I complied. After I had cleared most of my lungs, I looked up to see that we were already halfway across. I was lying across the Jaguar's back as the sky passed above! The sun was climbing to its zenith as a flock of herons flew over us.

*This is glorious!*

*Yes it is,* he thought. *But you're heavy! Tie the rope around your wrist and hold onto it with both hands.*

I complied.

*Now, lie down in the water as though you are sleeping. Let your ears sink below the surface and your face will float above. Keep your legs outstretched and straight. If you can manage it without sinking or choking, please kick those enormous feet of yours. It may not seem like it at first, but humans were born to swim just as surely as ja guars!*

I did as he asked, and the sky floated by. The sun was at midday when we landed at least a 1,000 paces down river from where we started on the opposite bank. My tunic was very heavy with water. I took it off and wrung it out in the river. Putting it back on my body cooled me. I fastened the rope we used around my waist.

*We'll have to take courage as we are bordering the territory of several other jaguars who have no interest in our safety. There's another spot upstream, but it's contested. You'll have to find a place to build within my territory, which is mostly downstream. Once the sun begins to touch the mountains in the west, we must be ready to depart.*

With that, I followed my protector into what he called his territory.

## 15

## THE PROTECTOR'S TERRITORY

The foliage on the other side of the river was much denser, with more shrubs among the trees, but the land was more level. *Pictures,* I thought. *Everything must be pictures.*

I began to make a picture in my mind of my old Dreaming Hut. I thought about its size and shape. I thought about the sheltered ridge where it stood.

*The land is flat here,* thought the Jaguar. *Better hunting!*

*Is there a place at the top of a hill or the crest of a ridge?*

*There is a high-place farther along, but we will have to turn back shortly after arriving.*

*Is there any way to be closer but higher?* I asked.

*Not where I can protect you.*

As we continued walking, the trees and shrubs began to give way to tall grass with larger patches of sunlight. The shadows shifted as the sun moved across the sky. After the sun was midway between its zenith and setting, I began to feel an upward slope underneath the grass. As the slope became more inclined, the dirt beneath began to be exposed. The Jaguar was expert at finding stones and other outcroppings on which to walk. He left very few footprints.

*Always tread lightly!* his thought thundered.

I looked back briefly. My path was far more visible than his, even through grass. I copied his footsteps as best I could. The top of the hill was crowned by a tree that was many times taller than a man. It's long branches and needles smelled of pine sap.

The Jaguar grunted. *Is this suitable?*

*Ideal, but far.*

*We shall have to be faster and earlier!*

There was a large bed of dried pine needles and cones below the tree's branches. I picked up a fallen branch and drew the outline of a new Dreaming Hut. I lay in the outline to confirm the size. It was perfect. Immediately after I stood, the Jaguar urinated in the middle of the circle. He then began to urinate all around the meadow surrounding the tree. His efforts reminded me that I needed to urinate as well.

As I began to lift my tunic, the Jaguar's thoughts interjected, *You must wait! My enemies will already be suspicious. I'll tell you where you can mark territory.*

A bit disappointed, I waited.

*Now we must return.*

I started back toward the way we came.

*We can't go back the way we came or the river will carry us to unknown banks. Follow close and move exactly as I do.*

We walked down along a sloping ridge line upstream veering away from the setting sun. Our pace was steady. Then the Jaguar stopped. I came up behind as silently as I was able. He sniffed at the air in utter silence. I tried to mimic, but I couldn't smell anything specific. All of those smells were new to me. He blew out his nose, and on a short grunt, moved downhill at an angle to the sloping ridge toward the river. The slope was steeper and much harder to navigate as the shadows lengthened and the light faded. Again, the cat stopped suddenly. I nearly ran into him. Again, he sniffed.

*We are at the edge of my territory,* he thought. *Drop!*

I complied with a sudden whoosh of breath. When I saw something move in the middle distance, I went lower.

*Stay on your feet, be prepared to move when I do!*

I wanted to ask what it was, but I didn't dare. A rumbling emerged in that same middle distance. I felt a rush through my mind, and I had to drop my hands to the ground to steady myself. I saw another image superimposed over what I saw with my eyes. In the second image, I saw the grass rustle as I had to steady myself again. Then I saw the Jaguar. I felt my consciousness split as I saw my protector from both the front and the back. A roar registered both in my own ears and from the middle distance. The second image left my consciousness as my own eyes saw another jaguar leap into the grass out of our path.

*You must remain still when I am still,* the Jaguar admonished.

*I tried, but I lost my balance when I saw from the other cat's eyes.*

*You're having visions?*

*No, I saw us.*

*You must maintain your discipline. Not all of our opponents will scare so easily.*

With that, he continued moving silently through the high grass that was in the process of turning from green to gold. As we came to the edge of the tree line, my Protector looked back at the path he had carved through the grass down the hill. There was a larger opening exposed where my crouching had nearly killed us. The Jaguar pointed his nose toward the path and the footprints underneath. I heard his breath change in rhythm. A wind rolled down from the top of the ridge and our path was erased.

The canopy of shadow was darker at this part of the river. The grass gave way to open dirt. The air was cooler and more moist. As we approached the bank, a deer and her fawn caught wind of us and scampered upstream back into the tall grass. The fawn knew enough to follow.

*Another meal missed, young one!*

*Can I piss here?*

*No! In the river.*

The current was swifter closer to this bank. I untied the rope at my waist and gave the end of it to the great cat.

*You remember how to cross the river?*

*Yes, Protector.*

*Good! Because I can't rescue you as easily here.*

I tied my end of the rope around my wrist just as before. As the Jaguar entered, I was pulled much more abruptly into the water. I quickly turned over on my back. As my head submerged briefly, I closed my eyes and mouth. Water seeped up my nose and began to sting, but I blew the water out as my face bobbed above the surface. The sun was setting and the whole of the sky was yielding to black in the east downstream. It was blue just east of the zenith and fading to purple further west. The hues of green changed to yellow, to red and back to orange as the ball of the sun skirted the edge of my view. Every time I saw a cloud, those layers of color were repeated in the contour of the cloud itself.

An alert serenity encapsulated me. I was floating

through Heaven at "The Crack Between the Worlds" as Uncle once called twilight. I knew I had seen it countless times before, but I had never contemplated the sky at such a magical moment. To this day, every time I see a river, my heart is filled with gratitude for having lived at such an instant.

UPON COMING to the opposite bank, the Jaguar dragged me out of the water. I pulled my tunic off and tried to wring it out again.

*Night is about to fall, young one, and you have a day of drinking and pissing ahead of you.* The Jaguar grunted for emphasis and turned toward the path to the Stone House. I flopped my wet tunic over my left shoulder when I saw a shaft of light from the setting sun illuminate the scars on my legs. The sight of them caused me to wince habitually, but I felt no pain. I could only hope that Uncle's herbs would have produced a similar cure. I turned around and followed the Jaguar up the path to the Stone House, the only home I could remember.

# 16

## THE MADNESS OF NECESSITY

Uncle's journey must have been difficult as he did not visit me that evening. The Jaguar kept vigil outside of the Stone House. The next morning, I was able to rise with the sun. The Jaguar greeted me, *You have your appointed duties, and I must leave.*

*I understand,* I thought. *I have a question. A delicate question.*

*I am not known for delicacy, but I will attempt an answer, young one.*

*Up to now, I think I've been able to keep you a secret from Uncle. Should I continue that secret?*

*I'm not sure you can, but if you are able, it would probably be easier for you.*

*Do you know my Uncle?*

*I will say that I am more acquainted with him than he is with me. However, memories are tricky, aren't they, young one? They are as much constructed as they are recorded. As you reconstruct your experiences in your old man's presence, it would be best if you left me out of your thoughts.*

*I understand. I must then ask you for a favor. I have discov-*

*ered that Uncle thinks of my thoughts only in words, but he cannot see pictures in my mind. After I follow Uncle's instructions and mark this territory, I ask that we no longer communicate in words.*

*At last! I find your words tedious. I only use these because you seem to prefer them! I wish you knew smells. Then we could communicate!*

*I don't think smells will work, but I think pictures will.*

*II think your old man's herbs interfere with many things in your unsmelled knowledge. Pictures it is! No more words then, so these will be my last to you until I hear otherwise. Your old man is not your kin! Look for me a few moments past the dawn.*

And with that, the Jaguar departed with some haste ahead of what I must admit was a pretty repugnant scent.

I BUILT a fire and retrieved the dishes I had used with the House Girl's herbs. I washed them as thoroughly as I could. Then I buried her herbs near where I found her Dreaming Hut.

I retrieved Uncle's herbs, and I brewed them in a tea and ate cornmeal. The tea's taste and smell were very strong. It was difficult to drink without gagging, so I drank more water out of the gourds that I filled. I brewed all the herbs at once, which meant the tea was very thick. I took in a mouthful of the dregs and instinctually spat them into the fire. A noxious smoke arose. I stood and backed away. I retrieved the pot while holding my nose. I then dumped the herbs several paces down the hill behind the Stone House.

As promised, I felt an incredible urge to urinate. I was surprised by how easily I was able to maintain my balance as I moved along the hillside marking my territory. I then scampered up the hill with incredible speed and agility. I felt like an antelope or a mountain goat. After returning to the fire pit, I filled the teacup again with cold water from a gourd and drank heartily. The smell, which was so repugnant before, had become pleasant to me, even inviting. It became pleasure itself. I spent the rest of the day running and drinking and urinating in an ecstatic frenzy. My thoughts were very narrow. I simply wanted to spread that scent.

It was nearly sunset when I remembered Uncle's instructions about urinating around the riverbank so thoroughly. However, I needed to take care not to get too close to the bank where I was to meet the Jaguar.

That night, I was very hungry. I ate two bowlfuls of Uncle's cornmeal and three pieces of jerky in a most compulsive manner. My mind became foggy. I stumbled into the Stone House. I don't remember if I properly doused the fire.

SLEEP WAS ALSO foggy and restless. A voice thundered through. It was Uncle.

*You used the herbs I left you.*

*Yes, Uncle. I am much recovered.*

*As it should be. I rest so that I may serve the Mighty-One in much haste. I will be there in five days at my current pace. Now rest yourself, Redcloud. The herbs will wear off, but the smell will keep the Cougar at bay until I return. All loyalty!*

*All loyalty!*

The absence of Uncle's thoughts gave way to a cascade of pictures. Pictures of the stars I had made, of Uncle's battles with the cougars. Images of the river, the washing, the site of the new hut, the site of the old hut. So much to do, so little time. So many questions! But, no words. I saw the

House Girl again, her long fingers against her beautiful, full lips. Her lips curling into a smile. A vision or a memory? No words! A stroke of lightning! A flash! I rose to the glow of the new star, fainter than before and more cloud-like. As I put my hands to my face, I could see light reflected back upon them. I closed one eye and then the other. The light diminished as I did this. Are my eyes glowing? No words! Questions prompted words! I scampered off behind the Stone House and relieved myself again, following instructions. These were good words.

*Following instructions, Uncle. Loyalty!*

As I WAS PEEING in the half-light, the images continued to flow until the stench I had spread came back to me. Uncle's tea must have been wearing off. Then it dawned on me. There was no way the Jaguar could stand to come ashore with this awful smell! How could I signal him? How could I meet him in the middle of a river?

I certainly wasn't experienced enough to swim out into the current just after daybreak. I thought of diving to catch a rope after having thrown it, but that seemed much too prone to fatal error. Anytime I let my thoughts drift back to the water, I felt a flash of the consumptive feeling I had when the Jaguar rescued me from drowning. The memory was scarier than the experience itself. It made me think of how little memory could actually reconstruct experience or perhaps how large experience was compared to our capacity to perceive it, let alone remember it.

Perhaps it was these weaving notions that brought a solution to crossing. I could fasten one end of the rope to something anchored to the riverbank and allow myself to float out into the current on my back. Of course, if I did that,

I would need another length of rope for the Jaguar to pull me to the other bank. A plan began to emerge.

I had to settle myself to make contact with the Jaguar. It was time to find calm and sing.

I sang the same tune I had used to make my Dreaming Body, but I substituted the word Jaguar as I sang it. At last, my breathing became more even.

*Greetings, young one! You said no more words, and yet you call me with your confounded jibber-jabber!*

*I don't know another way, and Uncle is otherwise occupied. He won't notice my thoughts,* I thought hopefully as my breath heaved again.

*How fortunate as I have a very important question. How are you going to cross the river without either of us dying?*

At this time, I relayed my plan for the next morning. His response was, *Well, at least I won't die!* He seemed to find this disturbing thought quite funny.

The next morning, I rose before the sun. The Jaguar would meet me soon. I pulled a second length of rope from behind the Stone House which I would have to replace when I returned, hoping Uncle wouldn't notice how wet it was.

I ate some jerky. The thought crossed my mind in pictures. I would have to devise a way to carry jerky with me to eat as I worked. It also would be better to keep the House Girl's herbs near the new Dreaming Hut as well. Perhaps I could use Uncle's smell-proof pouch? Was it enchanted? No questions! No words! No time for such things today. I filled the House Girl's pouch and two pieces of jerky and stuffed that pouch into Uncle's smell-proof pouch. As I ran down to the bank of the river, I fastened Uncle's pouch to the rope the Jaguar would use to drag me across. I also attached an empty gourd near the end of the rope so it would be easier to see.

The dawning sun cast sparse light over the pool from where we had left before. There was nothing secure to which I could attach the rope I would use to float into the current. The dense brush on either side of the pool obscured my view in both directions. I decided to walk upstream where the bank rose to a hill where I could no longer see the river. I climbed to the top of the hill to see a large willow tree growing. A large portion of the hill had been carried away by the current creating a small cliff where I could see a root structure growing into the river that seemed to be attached to the tree above. The dim light obscured my vision, but I was able to discern the cliff face. I strategized a way to navigate down to the roots safely. The cliff face was mostly loose soil, very dangerous when carrying two lengths of rope and an empty gourd, but there were some rocks to use as footholds. The willow tree had several low-lying branches I could hold on to as I started my descent.

As the sun grew brighter, the Jaguar was due to arrive. It was now or never. I grabbed the branches and slid down the cliff face. My left foot found the first rock. It was wide enough to take on my right foot as well. As I looked down the cliff, I reoriented my path and found some handholds. I was able to let go of the branches and make my way down to the log portion of the roots.

Going out farther, I found a section of root that was close enough to the water that I could knot one length of rope securely and still have enough length to meet the Jaguar safely (or so I supposed). I took the other end of the rope fastened to the branch and tied it loosely to my left wrist. I tied the end of the rope with the gourd attached around my right wrist. I wasn't sure how this configuration would affect my swimming, but I needed both hands to hold on to the rope attached to the roots until the Jaguar could make contact. I looped the coil of the gourd rope around my right shoulder; the gourd dangled from my side like ripe fruit. With ropes attached to both hands, I felt symmetrical for the madness that was about to come. In the distance, I saw the Jaguar. It was time. I lowered myself into the water and the current took me as expected. When the rope on my left hand was tight, I let the rope coiled around my right shoulder with the floating gourd attached loose.

*It's a good thing you stink , young one! I don't think I would have found you out here otherwise.* The Jaguar's thoughts brought relief. I felt the rope around my right wrist become tighter.

*Let go, boy!*

It took focused effort, but I managed to untie the rope attached to my left hand and let it dangle in the current. I hoped I would be able to find it on my return.

*Wait until we're in the current, then piss in the river. The smell will propel us faster!*

*No more words!* I thought.

*No more words, but I couldn't say that in pictures, and you don't know smell! ON!* the Jaguar roared with the rope in his teeth.

With the success of our launch, the Jaguar's swimming prowess brought us to the other shore in half the time as before. As usual, my tunic was soaked. As soon as I was able, I checked the pouch I had packed. It seemed to be intact. After I gathered the length of rope and the empty gourd, I shivered in the morning breeze. The Jaguar shook off the excess water from his fur, wetting me further.

*That's for the smell, you wretch!*

I smiled at the joke, but my shivering kept me from laughing.

*Perhaps you should take your bag off until it warms up a bit.*

I was not sure standing in my loincloth with the wind blowing on my wet skin was much of an improvement, but his reference to a bag gave me an idea. I removed my tunic and tied the belt rope around one end tightly enough to make a bag for gathering nuts. I attached the pouch to the bag. The Jaguar grunted his approval.

I filled the gourd and threw the rope over my shoulder. We made our way to the Dreaming Hut site. I stopped to gather as many piñon nuts as I could find. They became more plentiful as we began to go up hill.

We moved swiftly to the site, and I began to assemble the Dreaming Hut. I demonstrated to the Jaguar the kinds of branches I needed. He fetched them while I dug a hole to create a room underground. I had to be surrounded by the earth to travel in Dreams, although I don't think I knew that at the time. I was working off of the memory of image and instinct. I felt as though I had done this before or perhaps had helped someone else. Could it have been Uncle? No words here! Action!

The Jaguar was so adept at bringing up branches, I had to show him how to break them and put them into separate piles. When I needed to eat, I motioned the Jaguar toward Uncle's pouch. Even after rinsing it with some of the water from the gourd, he sniffed it briefly, then pulled away in disgust. I put the pouch down and began digging a hole four or five paces from the Dreaming Hut. I opened the pouch at the bottom of the hole and retrieved the jerky, which smelled of the House Girl's herbs. I closed Uncle's pouch as tightly as I could and buried it.

When it was time to return, I had begun to construct the

latticework for the top of the hut. However, I realized I would have to remove more dirt underneath to fit inside successfully. The Jaguar and I arrived at a wordless agreement that he would use his great paws the next day to dig the hole deeper. I retrieved Uncle's pouch and fastened it to the rope around my wrist.

On our journey back to the river bank, we encountered no opponents. The Jaguar urinated on the path prodigiously. After we entered the water, I peed. We crossed the river and the sun set in the same glorious fashion.

As we approached the other side, the Jaguar sneezed. *That scent is still revolting, but I think I can stand it long enough to get you on shore!*

The Jaguar roared as he dropped the rope after having dragged me ashore. I heard him slosh back into the water. I laid in the mud as the crickets filled my ears. Then I remembered that I had to erase all evidence of the Jaguar coming ashore before any of the prints dried. I filled up the gourd and splashed the water around enough to make it look like I had done some laundry.

My sandals and tunic were drenched and caked with dirt. It took all of my strength to wring out my tunic and loin cloth. As I put on my second one I thought, *At least I don't have to scrub that one.* I slipped on my sandals and inched toward the path to the Stone House. By the time I had gotten to the Stone House clearing, I was famished and ate three pieces of jerky. Sleep came easily once again.

THE NEXT MORNING, I used the House Girl's herbs spread on Uncle's jerky to heal my aching muscles. Clearer thinking and more practice meant for easier travels for the next three days.

Upon my next visit to the new site, the Jaguar had already dug out the rest of the foundation of the Dreaming Hut. After a day of trial and error at building a successful latticework , the rest of the construction went well. When it came to the point where it was ready to occupy, I was at a bit of a loss. I knew I had to go back to prepare for Uncle's arrival. There were far too few of my footprints. The Stone House needed to look, smell and feel as though it had been lived in for the previous twenty days. In all of that work, I never learned what the House Girl wanted me to do with the Dreaming Hut. I had become so consumed with building it, I didn't even consider why.

## 17

## THE PATH OF THE MIGHTY-ONE

Uncle looked much older when he returned. He arrived just before sundown. He had managed to carry two more large bags of dried corn. Even if he looked older, there was no doubting his stamina. As he placed the bags near the door, he said, "For grinding."

"Of course, Uncle."

He sat down as I reignited a cooking fire.

"I promised you a new house girl to do chores, but I'm afraid that is the first of many promises that I am likely to break."

"To my memory, this is the only promise you have broken, Uncle."

"Yes, I suppose you're right. In any case, the time has come for us to take steps into a new future, Redcloud. The Master is ready for His new conquest."

"New conquest?"

"Yes, Redcloud. Out of my loyalty to the Mighty-One, the King of Kings, I have discovered that this everyday world that you and I live in has grown too small for our King. His Power has outgrown it."

Night was falling, and Uncle's face became animated in a way I hadn't seen before.

He seemed playful, even impish. The flames danced across his cheeks as he explained why I had been making stars.

"You see, Redcloud, the Mighty-One has always been powerful. He has been powerful in a way that showed me that He was destined to rule these lands. When I saw this in Him, I knew that I must use my skills to benefit Him. Shortly after I met the King and became his ally, He gave me the strength to discover that I had a talent for learning ancestral knowledge. His Power showed me that I could see not only what had happened to me but also to my ancestors, and even in some cases, the ancestors of others. After I realized t his, I went back as far as I could in my Dreaming, and that's when I discovered it.

"Many generations in the past, my ancestors had learned how to speak to the stars. It took many years of intensive Dreaming to discover their methods, and by the time I learned how it was done, it was too late for me to learn the skill myself. There are many layers to our existence, Redcloud. Just as when you dig into the ground, you see different colors of earth, so it is true with experience itself. Certain layers can be seen only if you condition your body to see them. In order to talk to the stars, you can know only the layer of experience that can be seen through their light. To experience this, the whole of the body must be prepared as soon as possible after a child is born.

"The stars make destiny, Redcloud. They give the Mighty-One a world to rule so that those under him may be spared His wrath and be granted His mercy. When I told the Mighty-One my discovery, we began building the Crescent City with rooms that could never see the sun. Other Seers like myself also showed the Mighty-One how to build buildings that bring His subjects food for harvest at His command, how to control the rain and the snow and the thunder and even seize the sun itself! The projects were glorious indeed, but one by one, the Mighty-One's Seers failed to prove their loyalty. And, one by one, they were punished accordingly and now, I am the last."

"But what of the rooms? What of the children?"

"Ah, yes, we had created Darkness, He and I, then we had to fill it with those who could only know the light of the stars. At first, the Mighty-One told His subjects that they must sacrifice their children to our Darkness, if they didn't, the sun would not rise, and the rains would not come. Some of His subjects tried to flee or hide their children, and they were punished in due course. As we gathered them, the children were taken into Darkness and raised there. They were clothed and fed and reared all in Darkness. As we acquired more and more children, my Dreaming prowess grew. I learned how to Dream among them. This allowed me to teach the Songs my ancestors used to speak to the stars. When the children were grown enough to navigate a ladder and be led into the courtyard, we would take them out on the darkest night of the New Moon, and they sang as I listened. After doing this for a year, we would find an end to these Songs and wait in silence. On the longest, blackest night of the year, the children became star-talkers when they started singing the Songs taught to them by the stars themselves!

"At first, I would learn these songs and use them in my Dreaming later. This gave me the vision that the Mighty-One needed more children, but the real advance was when I learned to Dream awake as the Star-Talkers sang the new

Songs! I was flooded with visions! My mind was thick with them. It was then that the Mighty-One began to expand His territory to acquire ever more Star-Talkers. We built more and more cities like the Crescent City. The King's power seemed boundless. I became more adept at finding children who were especially suited to Star-Talking, and we prospered. And now, it is time to find yet more."

"More children?"

"Yes, Redcloud. Loyalty to the Mighty-One could make His need to find children in this world obsolete. The world in which you made the stars has countless millions to conquer and to cultivate! You see our new star here?"

"Of course, Uncle."

"It fades and dissipates. Its Songs have turned out to be poison. While poison would seem only to destroy, sometimes it exposes the heart of a matter. All is well, Redcloud. All is well because I have you."

"Me?"

*Me?!*

This was the first time I can remember my Uncle ever referring to my past. Sensing my disorientation, Uncle spoke to me in my mind.

*Yes, Redcloud, you.*

As questions began to mount, Uncle continued both in thought and voice. My only recourse to the onslaught was to breathe and receive.

"Each time the Star-Talkers sang a new Song, they told us where to go next for more children to spread the news of the Master's glory. When I met you as a young child, you were too old to train as a Star-Talker, and you were all alone.

I had assumed the Mighty-One had just dispatched your parents in His fashion."

Another sensation took over my consciousness. It was similar to how I felt as I had watched the Mighty-One kill the House Girl. It was raw and explosive, primal, and I still feel it to this day. I couldn't help myself. I asked, "I had parents?"

"Of course, you did!" Uncle replied.

"Why don't I remember them?"

He paused. "You didn't seem to want to remember what had happened to your parents when I found you. I don't know if you knew them or not. Your calm drew my attention. During the chaos that always accompanied the gathering of Star-Talkers, you simply stood in a clearing in the middle of the village. Your personae cleared my mind immediately. I began to See you in your energetic form. As we left, I collected you and kept you separate for the long march back to the Crescent City. As I had learned your language, you stayed near me. It was you who called me Uncle, but meeting you was just the beginning. As we marched back, I decided to raise you myself. When I brought you to the Stone House, our journeys to the other worlds began. You showed them to me."

Me? I was the one showing Uncle? I was the leader? I was too young then to ask the real questions.

He continued, "I sensed right away that you had a talent for Dreaming, so we built the Dreaming Hut, or rather you watched as I built."

My heart seethed, but I remained "loyal".

"You see, Redcloud, all of my Dreaming was about finding the core of the past. I Dreamed in the songs of old. You didn't Dream in songs at all. You Dreamed in pictures. We had to learn together, you and I. I taught you Songs to un-moor your Dreaming Body, and you brought back descriptions of these other worlds. It was a glorious time, but there was one world that became more and more solid to me every time you visited. This world became so solid that I was able to visit as an animal. I spent most of my time there as a crow. As we practiced together, we learned the Songs we have been using to make your stars.

"The world in which you make stars is particularly suited for the Mighty-One to conquer for the very reason it became easy to visit and to make stars. In that world, most people all believe in the same god."

Until he mentioned it, I had not considered one god over another. I had only some sense that there were gods and people believed in them although I couldn't say why.

"The Mighty-One's conquest must be absolute, so every time we harvested Star-Talkers from his subjects, He would make Himself their god. This proved to be tricky on occasion, even for the Mighty-One, but He always managed a way as one of His many talents. He started out with brute force. He would simply smash and burn all that was holy to the various villages. He would pillage their dead and uproot their holy relics and ancestors. When this tactic didn't work in a particular village, He was left with the arduous and inefficient task of slaughtering everyone. It was exhausting! As we became more proficient, the Mighty-One began to see the value not only of destruction but also of conjuring."

"Conjuring?"

"Yes. One of the last Seers to lose his loyalty revealed an ancient secret even more magnificent than speaking to stars. He taught the Mighty-One to make things through the sheer Intent of his Will. Indeed, the last two Crescent Cities required no labor to construct at all. They were simply Willed into existence by the Mighty-One Himself! They are the culmination of his practice of Intent. He started by Intending shrines to Himself and the making of bountiful harvests for the villagers. He would place these shrines in the same place where the villagers had built shrines to their old gods or ancestors. He became so proficient that He could do this before my very eyes and the eyes of His new subjects. Worship was inevitable and harvesting Star-Talkers became far less brutal and taxing, especially when the Mighty-One discovered that He would encounter far less resistance when I was allowed to be more selective.

"When we found your world, the prospect was simply too good to pass up. There was a whole new world to conquer. A vast world in which we only needed to supplant one god. Indeed, you stumbled onto the process of making stars as you explored this world. Its utter devotion to one, single thing made stars inevitable. You have a tremendous sensitivity, Redcloud. We only needed to Dream in the Mighty-One's presence, and you learned how to collapse the whole of a human being into one single point of existence. When you learned the Songs to do that, a star was born in an instant. You have made stars in places in this new world where energy was particularly oriented to one point and where there were individuals available whose energy was pliant enough to begin the process of collapse. Your skills and instincts in the process are awe-inspiring, Redcloud! You have my admiration and now, we must make one last star, so that the Mighty-One may go to this next world and conjure a temple to His glorious reign!"

"One more?"

"Yes, one more star. Then, you and I will show the Mighty-One the gate to the new world so that He may complete His conquest!"

"But my Dreaming Hut, it's destroyed."

"We must rebuild it, but that is the least of our worries."

"The least?"

"In order to create a gateway strong enough to allow the Mighty-One to pass, we're going to have to trap the Cougar that has been trying to kill you while you create the star!"

## 18

## SPLITTING THE CAT

I rose to find Uncle asleep. I couldn't tell if I had risen early, or if he had slept late. I made breakfast for us. I have more questions now than I did then. As I look back on this time, it seemed like I was in the river with the current pulling me wherever it would. Before I was being pulled by the House Girl's current. Now that Uncle had returned, I was in Uncle's current, and I was only beginning to learn how to swim to a bank. Some of what Uncle said had caused a stirring in me that felt familiar and frightening. Even if I acted on it, I was no match for Uncle or the Mighty-One at that time.

If Uncle was impressed by my newfound efficiency, he made no mention that I can recall after he rose. He ate with his usual impeccability. After we cleaned our dishes, Uncle began his instructions.

"First, we must repair your Dreaming Hut. It must be ready tonight."

We walked with the usual urgency to the site. I had forgotten how much damage had occurred.

"Start removing the branches," he commanded. We

spent the early morning clearing the hut down to the latticework of curved branches. "We'll be able to reuse most of this, but I'll need to find new lattice branches. Start breaking up these damaged pieces."

I obliged.

As the shadows grew shorter, I could hear branches being broken off the trees in the distance. Uncle returned and refashioned the damaged portion. I kept watch as to his design, so I could improve the Dreaming Hut I had built with the Jaguar. Mine was quite similar, but Uncle was more adept at crisscrossing the branches to hold the smaller sticks in place. I kept my thoughts on the matter as strictly pictorial as I was able, but I don't think it would have mattered. This was only the first item on our agenda for the day.

By the time the sun had come to its zenith, the latticework was ready to be filled in. Uncle demonstrated the technique of stacking sticks and branches. We moved forward with remarkable speed. As the sun began to grow large in the western sky, the Dreaming Hut had been completely reconstructed.

Immediately after we finished, Uncle took a pouch of herbs from his belt. He placed a pinch of the mixture in his mouth and took some water from the gourd he carried. He swished the mixture in his mouth as he walked to the far side of the new Dreaming Hut, then spat the mixture on the ground. He repeated this process four or five times right along the area I had urinated on six days previous. He looked at me intently. "The herbs I have spread here, Redcloud, will allow the Cougar to come back to you when you Dream tonight. If you hear him or sense his presence in some other way, you must stay in the Dreaming Hut for your protection."

"Is this hut an improvement over the last one that the Cougar destroyed?"

"No, it is not, but our strategy is different this time."

"What is our strategy? How is it different?" I said, trying not to sound frightened.

"Before, our purpose was entirely to fight off an invader. This time we must trap the Dreaming Body of the cougar. I know a maneuver that will do just that, but it will require all of my strength and concentration. I will not be able to defend you. Immediately after you make the star, you must return to this world. Here." He handed me a pouch. It was nearly empty and sealed tightly. "This is a more potent version of the herbs I gave you before. I will use the energy of your return to separate the Cougar's Dreaming Body from his physical one. When you return, you must open this pouch, chew on the herbs inside and spit the contents on the roof of your hut at my signal. The smell will drive away the cat's physical body, so I can trap the Dreaming Body. Here, take the rest of this gourd, so you'll be able to wet your mouth."

I took the gourd. "Yes, Uncle. I just wait in the hut?"

"Yes. Until I tell you to come out. After the Cougar is trapped, I must return to the Crescent City."

"You're leaving?"

"Yes, Redcloud. I'll have more instructions for you after our maneuver tonight. Let's go back to the Stone House and eat. We'll both need our strength."

I placed the pouch and the gourd Uncle had given me inside the Dreaming Hut where I knew I could reach them after my return. We walked back and ate cornmeal and jerky. Uncle encouraged me to drink even more water than I usually did. As I ate, Uncle spread another set of herbs over my cornmeal and said, "These herbs will show you a new kind of Power."

"Yes, Uncle."

"You will journey tonight to a city of sharp, polished stone next to rough, rounded stone. You will see more polished, white stone on the inside. Once you are inside, you will walk downstairs into the Earth twice."

We walked back to the Dreaming Hut. We arrived at dusk.

"Do you remember the Song for going into the other world and the one for coming back?"

"Of course, Uncle."

"You'll need to sing them with all your strength. I will not be able to help you tonight." He looked at the horizon. "I must go. I will return with my Dreaming Body to perform the maneuver. Remember my instructions."

"Yes, Uncle!"

Uncle scampered off into the looming darkness. As I entered my Dreaming Hut, I felt a new energy upon me.

I closed my eyes and began to sing.

~

*REDCLOUD! Lourdes interjected.*

*I hear you, Lourdes.*

*We can't allow your Uncle to succeed, thought Lourdes.*

*No. We can't, but we need to give the shadows their bait . They have to believe he has succeeded.*

*What shadows? What are you talking about? asked Lourdes.*

*I need you to learn the Song of Seeing, so you can See them. Uncle was a puppet to these shadows. He helped them rip a hole in the darkness showing the second sun, but such a burst of Power cannot be sustained. I know you have Seen before, but it was an accident, a fluke. Please be patient and watch as I learn. I will explain more as I return. Please know we can change this, but I need your discipline.*

*I don't even know what I'm looking for!*

*Please, thought Redcloud, stay calm. Watch for the time when the world waves as light and shape.*

*Do you mean during the explosions?*

*Yes. Seeing happens briefly when the stars are made, but what you're looking for is more controlled and more fluid. The Song of Seeing is different than the Song of Collapse, but they have a similar rhythm. I must continue in my journey. Please stay with me just a little longer, and we will learn the next steps together!*

*Learn? Lourdes asked. You don't know?*

*I've never died before. Have you? Redcloud's question sent them both back into his story.*

AT THE SAME point in the Song as before, I found myself in a great multitude of people. As Uncle had promised, the city was made of stone instead of metal. Looking before me, I saw a massive rounded building made of stone. It was much larger than the Crescent City itself. The stone blocks rose high into the air. Each wall was stacked with bricks half as tall as a man. The walls had openings within them where the stone bricks seemed to float at the top of a half-circle as other stone bricks came together at the top in an arch. This stone building was constructed as a circle of concentric arches stacked on top of each other some fourfold into the sky. Yet, despite all its majesty, the building was clearly a ruin. It stood as a decrepit, if impressive, stack of bones for what must have been an even more magnificent structure many generations ago. It was surrounded by the same smooth black stone and the rolling metal boxes I had seen before in this world, all still in a wretched hurry.

If I was visible to anyone in this city of stone, they made no mention of it. As my vision turned, I saw a group of women wearing fine robes of black and white. They each wore chains of gold around their necks with a golden cross elongated at the bottom. They walked into a much smaller building on a street adjacent to the rounded ruin that dominated my vision. The building the women entered was made of sharp, polished stone and my vision followed them. As they entered, each dipped her fingers into a bowl of water fastened to the wall next to the door at the entrance. Then they each made the same curious gesture.

Just as Uncle foretold, the inside of the building had some of the most beautiful polished stone I had ever seen. The stone was white with inlaid vines of gray. The robed women walked toward a shrine at the far side of the building, richly decorated with golden markings and ornate statues. In the center of the shrine, there was a sculpture of a young man in a loincloth. He looked similar to the inhabitants of the Crescent City, except that he was fastened by nails to two logs roped together to form a cross similar to the robed ladies' golden crosses.

My fascination with the colored glass decorations on the walls of the building nearly caused me to miss the movement of the women. My vision followed them down a set of stairs shaped like a twisted ladder into another shrine of rough stone. The far wall was also decorated but in a much more weathered and crude fashion than the shrine above. There was also a depiction of a man nailed to an elongated cross. Again, the women approached. Again, they gestured toward the shine. Again, they prayed. It was at this time I began to notice how many people were also inside this building. Many of them were children. I wondered if this is what the Rooms of Darkness might look like in the Crescent City. As the ladies rose from their prayer, I saw a younger one on the end begin to glow. She would be my prey. The ladies walked past my vision. My prey glowed ever brighter as she walked down a second set of twisted steps into a lower room.

This room was made of even more roughly hewn stone. There was a shrine at the far wall, but the ladies did not kneel. There was no cross on the wall as above. My prey began to glow ever brighter. I began the Song of Collapse out of sheer conditioning. I felt her burn and squeeze into a kernel of corn, then into a piece of dust. She glowed still brighter, then compressed in half, brighter, in half again, brighter still, in half yet again. The other people began to scream as the young one continued compression, in half, in half, and half again until a cacophony of Song and Collapse reached a peak of brightness, and the star was born!

This time, my escape was different. I felt my consciousness hurtle through stone and earth as they all burned into the essence of starlight. I saw the ladies disintegrate. I saw the children disintegrate. I saw their lives merge with the star.

As I began to sing the Song of Return, my mind superimposed images from the House Girl of the Mighty-One destroying her village, of his club smashing her skull. These traumas disturbed my Song, and my consciousness began to tumble out of control, a vision of the House Girl's face overtook my sensibilities. She put her finger to her mouth, and I found my Song again.

~

*No!* Lourdes shouted through the chaos. *The Giant can't come back! He's dead. He has to rest. That's what we agreed!*

*I know,* Redcloud responded.

*Will this bring him back?* asked Lourdes.

*I don't know. It's what they want, the Dark Creatures.*

*Why? It's not what the Giant wanted. Who are these Dark Creatures?*

*They are lonely and frightened. They think the Giant can help them. At least that's what I'm guessing. They live apart from us but among us. I'm just as confused as you are, but the only way to learn more is if you learn to See. I think my Uncle made contact with them in some way, but he never showed them to me. I can't think with you any longer. I must return. The lesson is coming!*

Lourdes found herself back in Redcloud's hut in a distant memory that was not her own.

THE LAST NOTE of my Song of Return was terminated by a loud growl and a smashing blow to the roof of the Dreaming Hut. I felt my eyes flash open. Another blow. It was at this time that I heard report of another animal to my right. It growled in a different register. The roof crackled under the weight of the Cougar. As I was not able to sit up, I rolled over and grabbed the gourd to my right and filled my mouth with water. I grabbed the pouch to my left and opened it as the growling continued. In the darkness, I took a large pinch of the foul-smelling herbs and placed it in my mouth and chewed. I felt some of the mixture pour out of my mouth, down my cheeks and past my ears.

Uncle's voice thundered in my mind, Now!

I spat the noxious fluid on the roof of the Dreaming Hut

with all my might. At the same time as there was a flash of light through the holes in the roof of the Dreaming Hut, I felt the cat's body leap off the hut . I hurriedly sucked more water into my mouth from the gourd. I dumped the remaining powdered herbs into my mouth and began to chew. Some of the powder fell into my nostrils, which began to burn. As I spat the mixture in my mouth onto the left-facing roof, another series of light flashes indicated some kind of struggle to my right. I rolled over to my right again and poured some water into the palm of my hand and attempted to wash the powder out of my nose. Initially, contact with the water made the burning worse, but when I sneezed, it brought some relief. I took more water in my mouth and swished it around as I felt my stomach begin to heave.

Another flash of light was accompanied by sounds I didn't understand, some kind of grunting and shuffling. After yet another flash of light, I turned to my left. Right after I spat out the water, I vomited. I rolled over again when I felt the vomiting spell subside. I took more water and continued to rinse my mouth. A few more bouts of rinsing settled my stomach. I could hear no more noises, but Uncle's instructions were clear, so I would stay in the hut until he signaled me.

I MUST HAVE FALLEN asleep because I saw daylight through the damaged roof as I opened my eyes. My first instinct was to drink the rest of the water in the gourd. With each gulp, the putrid smell of the Dreaming Hut got worse. I felt my stomach begin to heave again. I steadied my breathing long enough to listen outside. There were no unusual sounds. I turned over to see the shaft of light give report of midmorning at the opening of the Dreaming Hut about an arm's length above my head. A sneeze accompanied by another heave forced me to crawl out of the hut, signal or no.

Upon rising, I could see the footprints of the Cougar on the far-facing side of the Dreaming Hut. I turned around to look at the clearing where all the flashes of light came from. The sight was puzzling. The dirt was disheveled, as though there was a struggle, but there were no discernible footprints. My stomach twisted with hunger. I retrieved the gourd to find it empty. With instinct overtaking uncertainty, I walked straight to the riverbank, threw my head into the small pool where I retrieved the water in the past and drank heartily. I flushed out my nose and took some time to wash the vomit and dirt from my hair, then replaced my tunic with one I had "washed" on my return from the other side of the river. As I felt a surge of energy, I washed the tunic I Dreamed in the night before. Anytime I felt another pang of hunger, I drank from the pool. After hanging the cleaned tunic in a tree to dry, I walked back to the Stone House.

No fire had been built and nothing had been disturbed. I saw what must have been Uncle's footprints from the night before, but there were no footprints on the ground that had been made this morning. Then I saw another set of footprints that came out of the Stone House and led around the back. I opened the hide at the entrance. The Stone House was empty. Had Uncle left already? The footprints on the hard-crusted dirt of the floor were difficult to read. I took two pieces of jerky from a bag Uncle had brought and began gnawing, then placed one in my belt.

I followed the footprints leading out of the house. They took me down an overgrown path I had never seen before. It led into a mound of shrubs that I had passed countless times without ever having given it any thought. As I moved the shrubbery aside, I heard labored breathing. Stepping between two bushes, I nearly lost my balance as my foot stepped into the opening of another Dreaming Hut.

"Redcloud!" a raspy voice said. "I need water!" I carefully walked back and returned with a gourd.

"Help pull me out!" said Uncle with a tone of desperation I had never heard before. I reached inside and felt his calloused hands grip mine.

"Pull!" he said as his head emerged, and he sat up. I gave him the gourd, and he drank until he choked. I pulled the gourd away as I watched this shell of a man I knew as Uncle heave a few extra drops of water out of his lungs. He sounded like a wounded animal. After he composed himself, he drank more while remaining seated at the entrance to what I guessed was his Dreaming Hut.

He must have gone to great lengths to hide it from me although he could have just erased it from my memory. The path that led to it was not only hidden , but it was overgrown. Clearly, Uncle had not used this hut in some time.

"You performed brilliantly, Redcloud." A cough. "I captured the Cougar, and he is on his way to the Crescent City. Help me up. I must eat and start back. We cannot open the gate to the other world with my Dreaming Body alone."

"Yes, Uncle." I helped him to his feet and offered more water. He declined with a gesture and took my hand. I pulled him out of the hut and through the dense underbrush. We were both clumsy and noisy, a sensibility I found unnerving in Uncle's presence. He was ... weak.

We sat down as the sun was approaching its zenith. Uncle stared into the inactive fire pit, with no hint of smoke, as we ate jerky and drank water in silence .

After some time, he said, "Last night was a success, but a costly one."

"Will the Cougar return?" I asked.

"No. It will be lucky to survive the coming winter now that I have trapped its Dreaming Body."

"How did you do it?"

"Oh my, Redcloud, you are one of the most talented warriors I've ever come upon, but that technique will have to wait for another time."

"I didn't know there was a Dreaming Hut behind the Stone House."

He waved his hand nonchalantly. "I built it years before you came. I haven't used it since you arrived, but even warriors as experienced as myself need the succor of the Earth to execute such feats of Power as trapping the Dreaming Body of a cougar and a strong, young one at that!" He coughed briefly and drank more water.

He continued, "I must leave shortly after high sun. This is barely the halfway point of my plans."

"Halfway?"

"Yes. Now my Dreaming Body is carrying the Dreaming Body of that Cougar. I had to ask the Mighty-One Himself to enchant the bag I used. It is taxing to Dream away for such an extended period. I must reunite with my Dreaming Body as soon as possible.

"The rest of this maneuver must take place at the rising of the Blue Star ten days from now at the Sun Daggers. And you must be ready to Dream with us by then as well. The Mighty-One will use your loyalty to find His way through the gate that I open in concert with the Dreaming Body of the Cougar!"

"My loyalty?"

"Of course, you know how important loyalty is to the Mighty-One!"

"Yes, of course," I said with as much conviction as I could muster.

"Our services to Him are bearing their fruit. His glory is at hand!"

"Yes," seemed to be the only response available.

"Yes, indeed! Fill these gourds while I make preparations. I'll have more instructions when you return!"

I walked down to the pool to fill the gourds. I felt disoriented as I walked. Another image of the House Girl's face with her finger to her lips came over my consciousness as I entered the shade created by the tall cottonwoods at the bank. I filled the gourds.

Upon my return, Uncle had dressed and packed for traveling. Some of his characteristic vitality had returned. "Before I leave, I have instructions. I need to show you something else that you have never seen before. With that, he walked as I followed down the path toward his Medicine Hut. "The reason I haven't used that Dreaming Hut for so long, Redcloud, is because I have a different sensibility for warrior's work than you do. Instead of learning all of the intricacies of Dreaming, I spent more and more of my time learning about plants and animals. Such a specialty requires that I keep samples safe and at the ready. I know you've seen this hut from the outside. Now I must introduce you to the art of a Stalker.

"Your talents as a Dreamer are unrivaled, but some of these matters will likely be more difficult for you."

He stood at the entrance. "This Hut's location was not chosen idly. You must follow my instructions with total precision, or you could cause yourself and this whole desert grave injury. Do you understand?"

"Yes, Uncle."

As we stepped inside, it wasn't difficult to show wonder despite my familiarity with the interior. My physical body was capable of a different kind of sensation than my Dreaming Body.

"This Hut is built on top of a Place of Power," Uncle said. "You are never to linger here more than is necessary and sleeping here might kill you."

"Yes, Uncle."

"In five days, you must enter here at dawn when the Power here is most conducive to perform this maneuver. When do you enter?"

"In five days, at dawn."

"Yes. When you enter, on your right, you'll see this jade vase." He pointed to a vase made of green stone on a wooden shelf to the right of the entrance. "It will be glowing and provide light at the early hour. It only glows from first sight of the sun until the circle of the sun is fully exposed on the horizon. You must take this vase in your right hand. It may tingle or even burn your hand, but you must not drop it. It must stay in your right hand. Repeat!"

"I take the..."

"From the beginning!"

"In five days, at dawn, I will enter this hut. The jade vase will be glowing. I must take it in my right hand and take care not to drop it, even if it burns."

"Precisely! You will bring the vase to this table and hold it over this bowl." He gestured toward a bowl made of turquoise. "The bowl will begin to glow as well. Repeat!"

I repeated from the beginning.

"Then, with your left hand, take this pouch of herbs and powder next to the bowl. Repeat!"

Again, I repeated from the beginning.

"You will fill the bowl with the liquid inside the vase. Repeat!"

I repeated.

"Then, you must empty the contents of this pouch into the bowl with great haste and accuracy. If any of this mixture goes anywhere but this bowl, you'll start a fire and burn down everything around us. Repeat!"

I repeated with a new appreciation for repetitive accuracy.

"At that time, you must retreat to the Stone House until dawn the next day. You must move quickly with your head held high to keep from choking as you return to the house. Repeat!"

Again, I repeated.

We stepped outside. The sun was slightly past its zenith.

"I must make haste. I will not be able to call on you or protect you until you complete this maneuver in five days. Only then will I have the strength to relay the last of the instructions. In the name of the Mighty-One, we must succeed!"

I had no other thoughts as I watched him walk back down the trail to the Crescent City. I recall again marveling at Uncle's ability to find energy and purpose even after such an ordeal. I also recall the feeling that I had to follow those instructions. This is ingrained in my psyche to this very day. I also remember the feeling that my agenda would be much denser than Uncle could have known.

*That's Abuelito's vase!* Lourdes thought flickered.

*Yes*, Redcloud responded, *but the enemy is listening.*

## 19

# LESSONS IN POWER

With so much of the day gone, I had little choice but to attend to the many neglected chores. I filled all of the gourds. I ground corn. I replenished the firewood. I relished the taste of the fresh ground corn as my evening meal. I don't remember if I knew why I felt so compelled to cross the river again. I think I was still in a state of moral shock at what I had learned.

Having taken no herbs for the evening meal, my sleep was tumultuous despite my exhaustion. Images of burning buildings, burning huts and burning people passed through my consciousness. No amount of water seemed to quench my thirst that night. In frustration, I stood outside to breathe and steady my nerves. The pale blue of the new star confused dawn and dusk. The very fabric of being seemed to have a hole ripped into it. Any stars I would have known before were either obscured or shining from a new perspective. I stepped out into the clearing in front of the house to look to the east. The horizon was glowing orange. In spite of my efforts to the contrary, I thought, *It must be dawn.* I could only hope Uncle had already started his day and was too exhausted to notice my communication. It was time to make contact with the Jaguar. I began the Song that had called him before, but I must have sung it differently.

*You seem pained,* boomed the Jaguar's thoughts.

*No more and much less than others,* I replied.

*Others? The pain of others can be helpful if noted, but disastrous if indulged in,* thought the Jaguar.

*What if the pain is our own?*

*Are you still injured?*

*Only from my memories and thoughts,* I responded.

*Your old man did you a huge favor by stopping up memory. Still, if justice is your aim, memory is indispensable.*

*What is justice?*

*I thought you knew already. You must! I can't explain such things, but it's a notion that comes to my mind as we share our thoughts together.*

*We must meet again. I have to use the hut we made together.*

*That seemed like a lot of work just to make a pile in the forest.*

*I use it to Dream.*

*Aren't we doing that now?*

*These Dreams are different. At least I hope so.*

*You don't like this Dream?*

*No, I haven't been happy with the Dreams I've had in the Dreaming Hut Uncle built for me.*

*And you were hoping that by Dreaming in a new hut, your Dreams would be happier?*

*I don't know. I just know I need to be able to Dream separate from him.*

*Ah yes, your old man, the thought sniffer!*

*Yes. And you were right. He told me that he wasn't my real Uncle. He said I called him Uncle after he found me by myself in the middle of a burning village.*

*You are wise for being so young! Without his protection, you would have probably died.*

*Yes.*

*Were you able to keep your new hut a secret from him?* the Jaguar asked.

*I think so. He is not able to call on me for some time. He said I had a task to perform here in five days, but he did not tell me what to do with the rest of my time.*

*Ah! Free time! Wondrous!*

I told the Jaguar I could afford to spend two nights on the other side.

*Your mind is astonishing! The stench may actually be tolerable by now, but your contraption may be necessary. I'm on my way!*

I gathered the ropes, gourds and other supplies, then made my way down to the bank.

*Time to go!* the Jaguar announced his arrival.

I lowered myself into the current as the Jaguar swam out with the other end of the rope. This crossing was far more pleasant than the last. My senses seemed to be released from a layer of terror I hadn't noticed before. The air was sweeter. I began to indulge in the rolling sound of the current. We reached the other side. I felt as though I was ready to start a new life.

By the time we reached the unfinished Dreaming Hut, the sun was past its zenith, and my makeshift bag of damp nuts wasn't as full as I wanted it. I decided to explore the other side of the ridge as hunger trumped Dreaming at that moment. There were more trees, and I was able to double what I had found originally, but even with the jerky I had brought, this was going to be a lean two days if I didn't find more to eat.

Sensing my discomfort, the Jaguar asked, *How are your butchering skills, boy?*

They were negligible. While I had learned to use dishes and sticks to cook by watching the House Girl and Uncle, I had never handled meat beyond the jerky Uncle had given me and some fresh game and fish prepared by the House Girl. Uncle hadn't even taught me how to use a knife, let alone make one.

Again, sensing my thoughts, *I'll show you. I'm a bit of an expert on butchery, but I'm no cook. I'll hunt tonight. I'll eat my bits and bring back some for you.*

I thanked the Jaguar for having solved this problem for now. I went about making a fire pit away from the overhanging branches of the ponderosa pine above the shell of the Dreaming Hut. I then set about finding more fallen wood to make a fire. After all that effort, it dawned on me that I had no way to boil water to make tea for the House Girl's herbs. I decided I would have to sprinkle them over the nuts I had gathered or eat them plain with water.

With my chores multiplying, I asked the Jaguar, *Is there a spring or a stream nearer than the river bank?*

*There is, but it's half the distance to the river in another direction. It occasionally invites other residents of these woods, some savory and some not so. We'll have to leave now and move quickly if we are to return by sundown.*

With that, I used the length of rope to fasten my bag and the gourd about my waist. Haste made for a strange but workable configuration, and we were off.

The Jaguar picked its way through the wilderness with much more ease than I did. I struggled to maintain his pace and stopped whenever he did. At one point, I felt a certain surge of heat coming up from the ground. This prompted a question.

*Do you know anything about Places of Power?*

*Of course! How else would I survive?*

*How do you find them?*

*I made that mistake when I was young as well. There is no way to "find" a Place of Power. They find you, but there are all kinds of Power encountered in countless ways. Places have Power to be sure, but so do clouds and winds and animals. Power is not a "find"; it's a way. It's a sensibility for the process of existence. A sensibility that you have in abundance, I might add! You just sensed a Place of Power as we scampered past it just now. You summon it in your Songs. It's everywhere. For being so keen on protecting you, I think your old man has been very sparing with his knowledge of the world.*

At that, his thoughts stopped as did his movement. He crouched low. The grass below us was short. We were surrounded by the bushes of the chaparral that were transitioning to the grass in the lowlands below the ridge. The earth beneath my feet looked damp. We were near a water source. The Jaguar held his nose in the wind. I heard footsteps. There were two sets. The first set were those of at least two creatures, one was more careless than the other. The Jaguar brought his head low. I saw the Jaguar's thoughts. A deer and her fawn had passed by upwind. This image was followed by another thought.

*Wolves!*

I crouched even lower. That was the other set of footsteps I heard. If the wolves were stalking these deer, they would likely drive us away or even try to kill us. Still, not all animals behave as predicted. Of course, a wolf by itself was no match for the Jaguar, but an entire pack was another matter indeed. There was a sharp growl as one of the wolves pounced. The doe began running in the direction of the wind, which meant right toward us! The Jaguar leaped. *Follow!*

We ran perpendicular to the deer's path. The Jaguar ran straight into a wolf who was giving chase toward the deer from the side. The wolf yelped, but the Jaguar kept moving away from the deer. I followed, nearly tripping over the wolf myself. I saw another pass in the distance as the small pack descended on the fawn who was not able to escape with its mother. As we moved away, the Jaguar kept a pace he knew I could follow, which was faster than I had ever run in my life! He slowed, then stopped, then put his nose to the wind. I did the same. I didn't recognize any unusual scents, but the Jaguar was more cautious. He sniffed the ground and then the bark of a nearby tree. He promptly spun around and urinated on the trunk.

*Come! We'll need to quicken our pace. We'll move around the wolves.*

The noise of the pack consuming the fawn spurred a tense silence of thought between myself and the Jaguar. At least it was tense for me. As we approached a clearing with a spring-fed pond, the Jaguar roared, which frightened off some quail and rabbits. As both of us drank heartily, the Jaguar's thoughts returned.

*You asked about Places of Power. It should come as no surprise to you that you're in one now.*

*Now?* I replied.

*All springs are Places of Power.*

I looked to see the rock face to my left sweating with the fresh water we were now drinking. The taste was exquisite.

The Jaguar continued, *Places of Power are something that all creatures must be willing to cooperate around or die for because we all need them. It is very hard to keep them a secret except from those whose senses are so blunted that they may as well be made of air. You'll have to keep your wits about you after drinking this water. Its effects are unpredictable.*

I filled the gourd. We took a circular route back, which meant we had to increase our pace. Thankfully, the water was so invigorating, I was able to follow with minimal difficulty.

The sun was low on the horizon when we returned. I drank the water sparingly as the Jaguar cleaned himself languidly under the purple sky of the setting sun. I had only one piece of jerky left which I resolved to keep for breakfast. I reached for my tunic bag, pulled out some pine nuts and ate a few. Then, I remembered the House Girl's herbs. I dug up Uncle's pouch and pulled her herb pouch out. While I took care not to bring Uncle's pouch out of the hole, the Jaguar sneezed as I reburied the foul-smelling pouch. After I swallowed the nuts, I took some of the herbs and spread them onto my tongue. They had a fresh taste, almost sweet. I took another few nuts in my hand and sprinkled the herbs on the nuts and ate them. Were they not the last food within a day and a river's journey, I would have eaten them all. As it stood, I stopped after another two or three handfuls as the stars, including the new one, began punching the horizon.

*Damn that new star!* thundered the Jaguar. *It makes hunting much more difficult. He rose to his feet. I must go. I'll bring you meat,* he thought as he urinated around the perimeter, *but you'll need to leave the remains of a fire as you stay in your hut. Even if it is unfinished, the hut and the smell of the fire will keep most of the scavengers away!*

## 20

## THE SONG OF SEEING

A fire. I hadn't started a fire yet! As the Jaguar silently disappeared, I scrambled about in the last remaining sunlight to gather a fire-starting kit. I grabbed a handful of pine needles and placed them next to the fire pit I had made earlier. Then I found as many pieces of flat bark as I could although I could tell by the feel that they were probably too wet. Just as the sun ducked out of sight, I saw a dried branch from one of the cottonwood trees we had brought up from below when we started construction of the hut. I scurried around the Dreaming Hut and grabbed it just before the only light cast by the New Moon Sky was that of the mysterious "new star" and those of the more familiar old stars. Thankfully the air was relatively calm. I took some of the dried leaves from the cottonwood branch and made a small bed of kindling in the middle of the fire pit. I made a loose structure of dried pine needles on top of the leaves. That was the easy part.

I was able to break a stick off a branch about the same width as my middle finger. The wood was so dry that one end of the stick I broke off was relatively flat, a lucky break. I made it a suitable length for spinning. Without any flint or coals, I would have to make a spark with good old-fashioned sweat and effort. I chose the driest piece of bark I could find. It was about the length and width of my forearm. I placed it on the ground with the flat side facing me. I then put my feet on the ends of either side of the bark as I sat on the ground, my pose resembled a rabbit about to hop. I took the stick and held it upright on the flattest, driest part of the bark. I moved my hands to hold the other end of the stick between my palms with my fingers extended as though praying. I then moved my hands back and forth as though I was attempting to warm myself in cold weather. This motion caused the flat end of the stick to spin back and forth into the flat surface of the bark.

While I had seen the House Girl do this countless times, it proved much more difficult than I expected. As I had no choice, I persevered. After several attempts, I was able to keep the stick perpendicular as it spun back and forth against the bark as though an arrow had shot it while my feet held the bark in place. The spinning motion became more rhythmic and faster into the bark.

After some time and concentrated spinning, I checked the end of the stick rubbing against the bark. It was certainly hot, but it was not enough to ignite any dried leaves. I took a deep breath and resumed my efforts. I found my efficiency improved as I timed my hand motions in rhythm with my breathing. A Song of Fire-making began to emerge as I started to feel a machine-like efficiency in my aching hands. I continued for another run of spinning. I stopped briefly to put some crushed dried leaves on the surface of the bark where an indentation was starting to grow. After another round of spinning and breathing and Singing with more crushed leaves, I started to smell smoke.

I took another handful of crushed leaves and continued breathing and spinning with daemon-like efficiency. A spark ignited. I kept spinning as the spark became more consistent. As I continued my evolving Song, I put the hot end of the stick toward the outside of the fire pit and then I carefully dumped the sparking leaves on top of the tinder I had placed earlier. I then gently leaned over and started blowing on the sparks in rhythm with my Song. My heart soared when the fire ignited!

I built the fire fairly large, then ate another few handfuls of the herb-nut mixture and drank water, probably more than was prudent. As I looked into the fire, my breathing began to take on the rhythm I had achieved while making the spark. The rhythm became voiced as my posture straightened. I started taking breaths twice as long to sustain the panting notes into a clearer pattern. I then thrust my diaphragm down past my stomach into the pit of my pelvis and resumed the Song as I watched the fire. I began to Dream. Unable to stop myself, my consciousness began to move.

I FORCED MYSELF INTO A STEADY, deep breath I had used to make the spark. I opened what I thought were my eyes, but even now I find it difficult to describe. I knew it was still night, but the world was glowing. The light was as though I had awoken with a deep afternoon sun flooding my field of vision from all directions, not just the sky. No, it was flooding more than my vision. It was flooding all of my senses at the same time. The ground beneath me was singing. I smelled the ember burn in the same manner that I tasted the light of the dispersed star overhead.

*What is happening to me?* I thought.

This time, there was no response. There was no Uncle. There was no House Girl. There was no Jaguar. I was alone in my Dreams for the first time I could remember.

As my consciousness came into shape, outlines of the shrubbery in the clearing where I sat next to the fire began to take shape, but that shape was assumed by countless streams of light. The streams looked like animal fur surrounding the objects. Even as the shapes of the clearing took further hold, their brightness continued as though they were made of sunlight itself. While my body seemed to remain still, my consciousness spun around to see the glowing patch of the unfinished Dreaming Hut. Its brightness felt more saturated than the rest of the ground surrounding it.

I saw the giant pine tree above as it glowed sun-like. My consciousness spun again. All at once, a glowing vision of the Dreaming Hut I had watched Uncle rebuild became superimposed on the spot where my new one was to be. My steady breathing seemed to force the sticks and branches the Jaguar and I had gathered into the superimposed vision of the finished Dreaming Hut. Each new breath saw the larger branches lying crisscross on a latticework shell. Then smaller sticks and branches rose in their luminosity to break and form a shell of protection that would make the hut seem to be a fallen log, long covered, to the untrained eye. The opening was expertly hidden just as Uncle's had been. The vision of the old hut was being consumed by the actuality of the new hut with each passing breath.

*This must be conjuring!* I thought as my breath heaved in triumph causing the construction to halt on the last bit of dirt. I resumed my previous pattern and the dirt settled back into place.

My consciousness spun to face the fire I had lit.

Suddenly, the light of the fire coalesced into the face of the House Girl as it danced in the billows of heated air above the flames. She gestured with her lips toward the Dreaming Hut. My consciousness returned to my physical body, which continued to breathe at the fire. I rose to my feet and took up my gourd. The night had returned as the side of the Dreaming Hut undulated in the light of the flames. I stepped to the entrance and lay down inside it.

As I LAY DOWN, I began singing the Song I started at the fire. I felt a new lightness, a sense of liberty. As before, anything I thought of came to pass. Unlike before, there was no one to protect me from myself. My Dreaming Body floated above the Dreaming Hut. I saw the fire illuminating the tree from below. Then I shifted my perspective to see the same place but illuminated as it had been before. The tree, the Earth, the hut, all of them glowed in slightly different colors of light with all kinds of intensity.

*This must be how Uncle and the Jaguar see Places of Power,* I speculated, but then I remembered the Jaguar saying that Power went beyond place. My Dreaming Body soared high in the sky to see the whole of the Earth, and all of the sky also glowed with its own Power.

*Has this been here all along? Where's Uncle?*

At that thought, I spun like a shooting star into Uncle's mind. It seemed as if he was in a dreamless sleep. I felt the wisps of his memories that floated as light, thin clouds brushing the horizon high in the sky. Only now, these clouds were close. As I looked into one, I saw a conversation Uncle and I had together, only I saw it through his eyes. It was the last time we saw each other. His voice echoed in his own mind.

"I will not be able to call on you or protect you until you complete this maneuver in five days..." the thoughts beneath his words began to appear in my mind like ghosts of words and images as he spoke... *Yes, Redcloud, the Mighty-One will see the signal as a sign that he must go to the Daggers...*

I felt my breath heave as I rolled out of that memory back into the wispy clouded sky of Uncle's mind. I saw another more turbulent cloud. I was pulled toward it as though being pulled by the current of the river.

Now I was in a room of stone. When I saw Uncle's powerful hands, I knew I was seeing through his eyes again. Only this memory didn't have the same kind of echo the other cloud had. The memory seemed newer, clearer, more immediate. I saw Uncle was mixing crushed herbs and soil to make paint. I heard him quietly singing a Song I had never heard before. He became distracted when a bag shuffled in the corner.

*Patience my friend,* he thought, *your time is coming.* He continued working. I felt another burst of acceleration as I fell out of that memory. On the way out, I saw Uncle walking with that bag as he sang continuously. A wider perspective showed that this was the path to the Crescent City. His shoulders swung like a roped stone hanging from a tree, caught in a wind. There was Power in his stride, but it was the kind of Power that could unravel at any moment. The bag he was carrying seemed to be responding to its own set of rules as though it was blown by its own wind. It must have been the bag in which he carried the Dreaming Body of the Cougar. Another thought whisked by as I rose further away from this scene. I fell up, up into Uncle's sky.

*Rest at last!* Uncle's thoughts thundered in his sky. *As the Master moves on, peace shall reign! Rest! There must be rest!*

HE CONTINUED WORKING. I felt another burst of acceleration as I fell out of that memory. On the way out, I saw Uncle walking with that bag as he sang continuously. A wider perspective showed that this was the path to the Crescent City. His shoulders swung like a roped stone hanging from a tree, caught in a wind. There was Power in his stride, but it was the kind of Power that could unravel at any moment. The bag he was carrying seemed to be responding to its own set of rules as though it was blown by its own wind. It must have been the bag in which he carried the Dreaming Body of the Cougar. Another thought whisked by as I rose further away from this scene. I fell up, up into Uncle's sky.

As the smoke coursed from the torch, I saw a face of helplessness that seemed incongruous on the Mighty-One's body. Another shriek from Uncle, *You destroyed my village! You murdered my people! You burned my parents!* Each thought punctuated by another shriek, which pushed the Mighty-One another step back. Each shriek pounded another layer of defiance into his enormous face.

The Mighty-One roared, "No one defies me!" The torch reignited as another swing brought it down toward Uncle's head. Another shriek dissipated the blow again.

His confidence intact, the Mighty-One switched his approach. With another blow forward he said, "You are strong! You can control fear!" The blow stopped as he stepped back suddenly. He extended his torch to point it directly at Uncle's face. The Mighty-One's face rippled through the heat of the torch. "You must be my ally!" I felt a sense of shock at this sudden turn. "I am a Man of Power beyond all other men! I have dominated all who cross my path. Only those who remain loyal will survive!"

Another layer of screams emanated from somewhere in the village. The Mighty-One swung the torch again, smashing a nearby hut. "Your loyalty will spare the rest of this village and any others you desire!" He raised the torch upright toward this sky of memory. The Giant looked directly into Uncle's eyes, into my eyes. The core of my being began to tingle uncomfortably. He bent down to bring his enormous face close to ours. "When I snap my fingers, you will fall asleep but remain standing with your eyes open. You will only hear my voice." He raised his massive hand next to our face and snapped his gigantic fingers. "You will pledge absolute fealty, love and loyalty to me. Repeat!"

There was another snap of his fingers as I heard Uncle say, "I pledge absolute fealty, love and loyalty to you." *This is not my mind!* I thought. *I will not repeat!* I felt compelled to fight with every fiber of my being. *I will not repeat!*

"You will be my ally, and you will do my bidding. Repeat!" Another snap of the fingers next to the face. The thunder cracked in Uncle's mind as well as my own.

"I will be your ally, and I will do your bidding," Uncle dutifully intoned.

"I can never be defeated. I can only be joined. Repeat!" A snap.

"You can never be defeated. You can only be joined." *RESIST!* I begged of myself.

"I am all Powerful. Repeat!" Snap.

"You are all Powerful."

"I am all Merciful. Repeat!" Snap.

"You are all Merciful."

"I am your Lord and Master! Repeat!" Snap.

"You are my Lord and Master!"

"I am your Almighty God! Repeat!" Snap.

"You are my Almighty God!"

"You will have no memory or attachment to this place! Repeat!" Another snap. Another repeat, this time with more uniformity and calm, almost docility. Uncle seemed to be relieved to forget.

"You will only remember your loyalty to me! Repeat!" Snap. Uncle repeated again in an even tone.

"When I clap my hands, you will be awake and ready for your new challenges at my command!" He clapped his hands together.

As Uncle's consciousness returned, I was exhausted with this memory, but Uncle remembered nothing. He said, "How may I serve you Oh, Mighty-One!"

"Come," said the Giant, "we have business."

*Peace!* Uncle's thoughts raged underneath the memory. *Oh, Master, there must be peace!*

Again, I fell backward through the smoke into the "sky."

THIS TIME, it was Redcloud who called to Lourdes. *Did you hear the Song of Seeing?*

*Yes,* she replied.

*We have a moment here to look at my memory of my Uncle, but we must be brief. Sing with me!*

Lourdes sang along with Redcloud the Song of Seeing. Her consciousness returned to the scene in which the Giant was asking Uncle to repeat. Only now, the Song of Seeing caused the memory to be bathed in the light Lourdes had seen when Redcloud built his hut. As they continued their Song, Redcloud and Lourdes pulled farther away. At every moment the Giant snapped his fingers, sparks of energy flew at the sound. The sparks created a shower in which splotches of darkness appeared. At every snap, the splotches became more distinct and numerous.

*Do you See them now?* Redcloud asked.

*Yes.*

Another snap caused more creatures to appear.

Redcloud continued, *They don't seem to eat food as we do. They are not made of sunlight as we are, but I know they are alive all the same.*

*Are they Dark Matter?* Lourdes asked.

*I'm not sure what that is, but it sounds as correct as any way I have heard them described. They seem to need us.*

Another snap. More Dark Creatures appeared.

*They seem to need our light*, thought Redcloud. *It is their food.*

*Then the Giant is helping them?*

*In a manner of speaking, he is unaware of them as he does this. Most of us are unaware. I didn't find them until much later in my life. My observations have shown me that they need devotion. They need attention, and your one God has created a bottleneck for their sustenance. In your time, these creatures must gather at the Holy sites in which I created stars. In trying to rid his time of the Giant, Uncle was also setting these creatures loose in your time.*

*If they do not believe they have succeeded,* Lourdes continued the thought, *they will find another way. Do they have to harm us to get what they need?* Lourdes asked.

*I don't know, but they have Power. Anything deprived of Power to sustain itself can become dangerous. Our defeat of the Giant was a defeat for a group of these creatures who did not want to get their sustenance from those who control attention to your deity in your time. I believe they will continue their quest unless they are all destroyed.*

Lourdes' Song wavered, and her vision of Redcloud's memory began to slip. Still, she felt a connection to Redcloud. Enough to ask one more question. *So, in saving all those people, our people, we're causing these creatures to starve in our time?*

*Perhaps. But we can't allow them to destroy your world.*

*No. We can't. And you're dying. How am I going to deal with them without you?* Lourdes' question caused her consciousness to re-merge with Redcloud's recapitulation.

## 21

## THE SONG OF THE MONSTER

The sensation of moving backward continued as my Song continued. Occasionally, I was buffeted from side to side in the tumult of Uncle's mind. For being a man of such pure physical discipline, it was confusing to find his mind so disorderly. Perhaps that's why he had trouble focusing his vision in Dreams. As I fell backward, I felt a sudden updraft that caused my so-called stomach to drop. I felt a sudden spray against my face, then began to plummet. I had to keep reminding myself that there was no ground in the mind, or at least I hoped there wasn't. At this very notion, I began to see treetops racing below me coming up behind as though I were some kind of mad backward-flying bird above the forest. As I charged into the leaves, I began to relax when I discovered that my body wasn't solid in this Dream.

The smell of smoke emerged again. Uncle's vision came to overlook a small village. My consciousness twitched with unnerving familiarity as I felt his feet touch the ground. A breeze flowed through the jet-black hair of a young Uncle. I felt a fierce focus in his musculature as his eyes fell upon a small child standing in a clearing.

I began to feel the intensity of the Song in my Dreaming Hut increase as my heartbeat began to pound.

Uncle looked to his side as the Mighty-One approached. To his other side, another identical Mighty-One appeared. Both were carrying torches, both breathed with an easy thunder. A phalanx of perhaps ten warriors moved in on either side. All carried torches. After war-whoops, the twenty warriors threw their torches. The whoops caused a part of my consciousness to crack. I felt tears begin to flow on my physical body in the Dreaming Hut, causing Uncle's vision to blur in my mind.

As the Mighty-One and his double entered the village, Uncle's vision changed to Seeing. His breathing was an echo of my own Song. His was a silent Song of Seeing the Earth as the daughter of the Sun. The Song was the Sun's rightful heir to the Power of the cosmos.

The shapes of the huts became visible in Uncle's Seeing vision. The fires beginning to catch in the huts revealed the shimmering horror of burning children and howling parents. This reminded me of the last time I had made a star. There was no escaping my culpability. I was every bit the monster that the Mighty-One or my Uncle ever were.

Uncle's vision however seemed to be just as immune to these terrors as mine had once been. He had a task. If he failed in the slightest, he would surely be killed just as many of his colleagues had. *No time for pity; only Star-Talkers will suffice*! he thought as his vision focused on infants. He would wave his muscular hands and the babies would be snatched by the marauders. Their parents were dispatched without pause. Until he came upon me ...

My physical body lurched back to consciousness as my Song became a shriek. I backed out of the Dreaming Hut to have my head emerge the way an ant would emerge from its hole. My insides felt a tingling numbness. My eyes were drawn to the most immediate source of light in the perpetual twilight of the fading new star. The low flame of the fire I had built was pulsating with my breath, which had lost all semblance of cogent rhythm.

Had my so-called Uncle murdered my parents? What did he see in me? Why was I so special?

I heard something being dragged outside the light cast by the fire as my questions ceased.

*It's a damned good thing this doe was already dead when you shrieked in the night, young one!* The Jaguar's thoughts caused a change in the rhythm of my breath.

*He stole me!* I replied. *The old man, he stole me from my family. He probably had them killed right after he took me.*

*Ah! Family! I have not seen my family either. How did you find this Young One?*

*I saw the attack on my village when I was young. I saw infants slaughtered, their parents burned and killed.*

*You saw this in your own memories?*

*I saw it in my... the old man's memories.*

*You saw yourself through his memories?*

*No. I got scared. That was the shriek you heard.*

*If you have found a way to enter his memories, then you must go back, young one.*

*Go back?* I replied.

*Of course! The Great Spirit does not dole out such opportunities lightly. You have an immense advantage if you can see your-*

*self through the eyes of another, especially a highly skilled warrior such as your old man.*

*No! No! I can't. He's taught me to kill innocent people.*

*Yes, killing innocence is hard to move through. It must be, in order to maintain respect for your own life. Even this doe we will eat suffered the burden of innocence, and I, the burden of killing her.*

*Yes, but we're going to eat her. There is Justice in that!*

*Ha! Justice! Yes! I knew you knew what it was. And now you feel your old man has been unjust in his treatment of you, of your family, and you, of course, are justified in your feelings. But remember this. He, too, feels justified in his feelings and his actions. He finds Justice in his cause, just as this doe felt Justice in hers.*

*But there can never be Justice in mindless slaughter! My... old man didn't eat those people to stay alive. The people that I burnt to death while making those stars were no threat to me! I have been unjust. He has been unjust!*

*And who has been unjust to him?*

This thought jarred me. Again, I experienced a new kind of breathing. The Jaguar continued.

*One person's Justice seems another person's survival perhaps. Maybe there is no such thing as Justice. Maybe it's all just a matter of living and dying like some seeds landing on the rock and some in the river and some in the soil. Very few of those seeds actually grow into a plant. Is that Just? I don't know, young one. I don't know.*

*But we are alive. We know that*, I replied.

*Yes, and we all die. We know that too, or we ought to. Perhaps your old man's master has thought otherwise. Perhaps your old man entertains the notion that he will live forever as well. Perhaps that is the Ultimate Injustice.*

*What do you mean?*

*You must decide. We all must decide. Is our being alive an act of Justice or no? Is our death an act of Justice or no, because it seems that living and dying must be the same action, or there can be no such thing as Justice? What if your family survived the burning of your village? Would that make the action just or unjust? What if this doe lived on even after we ate her? How would that change the nature of Justice for her? Perhaps she does live on only if we eat her. Are we her arbiters of Justice?*

*So, if I kill my old man, in discovering his own mortality, he can know his Justice?*

*You're asking me?*

*Yes.*

*I cannot answer that question for anybody but myself. Killing your old man would not be any act of Justice for me at this time.*

*Why do you protect me?*

*Because keeping you alive is an act of Justice for me at this time, perhaps for all time! Now, it is Just that you eat and sleep, and sleep out in the open. I'll watch you. That shriek nearly killed me.*

# 22

# INVASIONS

I slept until late morning. Cutting the corpse of the doe proved to be unworkable as I didn't have a knife, didn't know how to make one and wasn't sure what to cut. Another injustice? I ate more nuts with herbs and found myself still quite hungry. The Jaguar's response was, *More for me! Go find your twigs, but stay where I can hear you.*

I took my tunic bag and walked into the brush, looking for more nuts or anything else that might pass for food. I was so loud and smelly that I probably scared off anything that could harm me. It was also about this time I started to take stock of what Un ... the old man hadn't taught me. How could I not know how to use a knife to prepare meat? The more I thought about how much I needed him, the more frightened I became. If he came to harm, what would I do? The night before, I was contemplating killing him. I might as well have killed myself. All my feelings for him were based on my truncated memories and a basket of habits continuing my need for him. The Jaguar was right. I had to summon the strength to re-enter his mind and see myself with his eyes. I would have to maintain my composure no matter my hunger or fear.

I wondered if he would have any memory of my foray into his memories. Would I have known if he had looked into my memories? Would anybody? At last! I found a tree that hadn't dropped all of its seeds yet. As I picked through the cones, the bottom of my bag began to fill. At least I wouldn't be completely hungry.

When I returned to the clearing at the top of the ridge, the Jaguar had already dragged off the carcass, taking the gathering flies with it.

*You'll never know what you're missing, young one. Nothing rolls off the teeth better than fresh flesh!*

I heard him eating just out of sight down the hillside.

*You're right,* I replied. *I have to go back to the old man's memories. Although I'm not really sure how I got there in the first place.*

*Will!* he thundered. *Will is the only way to get anywhere, especially in Dreams. Will, my friend is deceptively simple. Focused Will, that is what you have begun to master. You will re-enter his memory by simply insisting on it. That's how you did it before because that is how it is always done!*

*I remember now,* I replied. *I remember I started a new Song last night when I created the spark that started the fire. I could do that again.*

*The logic of repetition doesn't always work in Dreams, but I suppose it will have to do.*

*I'll have to cross the river again as close to dawn as possible tomorrow.*

*Yes! I love a good swim at dawn!*

As the sun began to set, I went about the motions of creating a new spark as the Jaguar looked on. Even as the coals from the previous night smoldered, the new Song returned as my breath achieved the sublime rhythm.

ONCE AGAIN, the darkening world was bathed in glorious sunlight. As soon as my consciousness attenuated to this level, I rose and entered the Dreaming Hut. Once again, I asked to find Uncle, but that was the last thing that was the same.

*Redcloud!* Uncle thundered hollowly. *You must return to your body at once! We cannot Dream together at this time!*

*A thousand pardons, Uncle, I didn't know I had traveled to you.*

*You are becoming careless at a time when you must take more care than ever! Go now!*

I felt myself being pushed away feebly from the old man's consciousness like an unwanted puppy. How did he see me now and not before? Perhaps he hadn't slept yet, or perhaps he no longer needed to contain the Cougar. I couldn't know until I waited. Something else that was different, as I heard Uncle's thoughts, the world ceased to be illuminated. I had lost my Song.

I tried to reestablish control by returning to my physical body. I resumed my breath with the same kind of intensity. As the Song came back to me, the world became illuminated once again. My consciousness soared. Then it occurred to me that I might have to wait for Uncle's mind to become more pliable, perhaps I could learn more about my own mind. If I could find my own memory of the event, I might be able to sidestep Uncle's attention and re-enter his perception of this memory from my own. Didn't the Jaguar say that everything in Dreams is done through Will?

At that thought, I began to feel myself flying backward again. Only this time, instead of clouds, everything continued in a state of luminescence. Everything essentially looked the same. There were no objects to distinguish. There was no sky. There were no clouds.

*No more light!* I thought in frustration. At which point, everything became darkness as I continued flowing backward. Where was I? Where did I need to go? Then I remembered the smallness of my body in the memory from the night before. I felt my form become compact in the manner of a child. I closed my Dreaming eyes and opened them to see the world as light again.

*Meeting Uncle!* My thoughts shouted as I closed my Dreaming eyes once more. Upon opening them, I smelled the smoke I had smelled before. It was that bitter, bitter, cloudy day when I met Uncle. The flames had made my condensing body hot. I pulled my Dreaming hands up to inspect them. Instinct told me that I had arrived at the memory.

The flames licked at the buildings. I began to choke on the smoke. I felt a shadow dominate my field of vision as I looked to the side. I felt my diaphragm sink into the pit of my guts. I turned to face this shadow. It had no face, no features. My heart stirred as my recollection triggered a heave in my breath. I hurled all of my energy in the direction of the shadow. Then the Song I had begun at the fire overcame my younger body as I began to Sing it in the Dream. As I watched the world transform, I recognized Uncle's younger face.

All at once, I saw the world as sunlight again. I looked at the man I would call Uncle. He seemed to glow in an orb very much like a star. As I sang my Song more forcefully, I felt myself moving toward the orb. Getting "closer," I started to see more features locked inside. When I came to the edge of the orb, I felt myself as an orb of light as well.

*To the blue sky!* I shouted in The Dream. At that moment, I thrust forward into a blue sky. This sky, however, was distinctly different than the one I encountered in Uncle's memory before. As a cloud floated by to reveal the ground underneath, I found that I was in an actual blue sky (whatever that was in a Dream).

*Focus! Details!* I thought.

*Uncle's blue sky of memories!* I shouted. This time, I felt myself being thrust backward. The clouds of the actual sky brushed past until I heard my Song being sung again in my hut. All the world became sunlight again. Then, at last, I arrived at the oddly familiar sky, bright and blue, but no sun to speak of. Perhaps my body itself was the sun in this sky. I moved backward as before. The clouds passed by me as I thought of myself in that compact form as a child. As I look back now, this is the first childhood memory I can construct. As before, a burst of acceleration through gray clouds becoming smoke. Only now, instead of seeing my hands attached to that small body, I saw Uncle's hands as I looked up to see Uncle's memory of me. I felt Uncle's consciousness shift within his memory and my physical breath heaved again as the world became as bright as a flash. Was this part of Uncle's memory, or was I breaking away again? I made the choice that it must be part of Uncle's memory. I had to stay.

Peering back into the flash, I realized that Uncle was as shocked by it as I was. His vision came back to the physical world in a way that stunned his sensibilities. Another flash hit this memory again. Once more, it seemed to come completely from my body as a child. I was defending myself!

Uncle gestured to a few warriors in his midst to attack me. He shouted in what must have been their language to take me. I flashed again knocking two of them over. Uncle then reached for a pouch tied to his belt as he fended off another of my flashes. He pulled out a tube of bone about the length of his hand that was hollow. Another flash. He blew through the tube. I felt a tingling as his breathing deviated. He pulled out another smaller solid wooden shaft with a notch cut into one end. Another flash. As his eyesight returned, he found a small arrowhead which he slid into the notch on the wooden shaft. The shaft then neatly slid into the tube. He held the tube and the shaft in his left hand and reached for another pouch attached to his belt.

Another flash took him off guard, and he stumbled slightly as some of the powder in the pouch spilled onto his fingers. At the touch of the powder, his fingers began to tingle and become numb. Another flash. While he kept his footing steadier, it took all his concentration to dip the small arrowhead into his pouch and close it. He did all this while his left hand was beginning to feel like a club.

As another flash hit him, he turned his back to me. He shouted at two warriors to run toward me. Another flash and Uncle started walking backward toward me.

*The man with no face!* My consciousness recoiled but maintained its hold on Uncle's perception of his memory. Another flash as he moved a few more paces back. When he saw the two warriors he had ordered to run at me fall backward, stunned again, he gripped the tube expertly in his right hand even as his left hand became dead weight. After the next flash, Uncle spun around and blew the dart. It hit me directly in the neck. The pain of it stung in my memory.

*Not now!* I thought. *Not yet!*

This time, there was another flash accompanied by a screech that forced Uncle to cover his ears, but his left hand was unresponsive to the command. His left ear continued ringing long after the screech had finished. Uncle's eyesight had also turned to a shade of purple. He managed to reach forward and pull the dart out of my neck just before I fell face first to the ground. This registered as the second of his many memories of saving my life.

Uncle ordered two more warriors to carry me out of his sight.

ALL SURVIVORS of the raid were gathered in a clearing outside of the village. There were about fifty people, most of them adolescents and young women. They were surrounded by a circle of warriors as the Mighty-One and his dark-faced double approached from opposite sides. Uncle also stood in the circle surrounding the frightened survivors. The Mighty-One addressed them. His words came from both of his mouths. He would start a sentence with one body and finish it or repeat it with the other. This seemed to cause further fright.

"You have made a bold and brave sacrifice this day. You have made this sacrifice to me, your Mighty-One! Now your village will be allowed to rebuild and prosper and grow. Your Mighty-One is here to protect you. I will see to it that the rains will come, your crops will flourish, and game will be plentiful during the hunt. Your god only demands two things of you. The first thing I demand is your complete and total loyalty to my benevolent reign. The second thing I demand is continued sacrifice in return for my continued mercy. With every harvest, your village will supply me and my representatives thirty bags of corn and three dead turkeys. The rest of the sacrifice will entail at least one child of my choosing born within two seasons of the harvest moon. If these things are provided, then all shall be well, and all shall prosper. If these things are not provided, then all shall suffer.

"You will bring your sacrifices to my temple, and you will bring them without fail! Behold!"

At that, the Mighty-One raised both sets of his arms as the earth started to shake under Uncle's feet. Some of the younger villagers screamed as a wall of stones began to rise in the circle between the crowd and the circle of invaders. The villagers started to sink within this circle as stones began to form bricks out of the soil that made up the sides of the circular pit that was then taking shape. The pit stopped sinking as the earth stopped shaking.

"This will be my temple!" the two voices thundered in unison. "You will build an appropriate structure to cover it and make it a place worthy of my mercy and Power. Now! Kneel before me!" The ground shook again causing many of the villagers to fall to their knees just as Uncle and all of the warriors surrounding the circular pit had already done at his command. The rest of the villagers began to kneel as the earth continued to shake and the pit grew deeper and deeper. It was now deep enough that none of the villagers could be seen from ground-level at a distance. As soon as every villager was kneeling, the earth stopped shaking. A series of branches flew through the air as though dangling from invisible strings. They elegantly formed themselves into a ladder as sinew from the wrecked village flew up and tied together the rungs and the sides of the ladder in a spectacular, if a bit anticlimactic , display of Power. As the ladder descended into the pit, the Mighty-One with his double declared, "Further evidence of my mercy and Power!"

Soon after the Mighty-One spoke, I felt my perspective flying backward again. Once more, the sunless blue sky surrounded me. I felt the rhythm of my breathing in the Dreaming Hut. Then, all became darkness.

## 23

# THE SIGNAL

I opened what seemed to be the eyes of my physical body only to see darkness. As I was about to let my eyes close again, I felt my head being nudged by a dark mass.

*Time to rise, young one! That's enough Dreaming for one night. We have a date with a swollen river!*

I reached out my hand to feel the furry side of the Jaguar's massive paw. I slid out of my Dreaming Hut. As my head emerged, the quarter-moon sky was still a-light as the star-cloud came into view.

I ate the remains of the nuts and buried the rest of the House Girl's herbs. There was only about half of the herbs left, but Uncle could never know I had them. I untied my tunic. The Jaguar led me down what might have been a familiar path in the sunlight. This time, it was slower going.

The red glow of the sun began peeking through the bushes as the path opened up underneath the taller cottonwoods.

In what was now a familiar routine, I attached my sandals, my gourd and my tunic to the rope. I then tied the end around my right wrist. The Jaguar took the other end of the rope. The sky grew brighter, with shades of crimson turning to blue as we crossed. The Jaguar dragged me ashore and quickly returned to the water.

*You have my profound thanks!* I thought.

*I'll be seeing you again, young one. Stay safe and stay wise!*

As soon as he left, I wiped away his footprints. I erased every other trace of my journeys. Then I filled the gourds and went up the trail to the Stone House, relieved to see it.

As soon as I entered, I began eating jerky. With each new bite, I reminded myself of Uncle's instructions. Enter the Medicine Hut, find the jade vase and the bowl, pour the mixture and leave the hut. I wondered what kind of signal Uncle was referring to.

I spent the rest of the day trying to make the area look like I had been there the last two days. I made footprints to familiar places. I was struck by just how little I traveled in a typical day. I saw the corn in the bag that Uncle had brought.

*Did this corn come from my village?* This thought caused a cascade that made my stomach sink. Is my village still there? Do I have any family? Real family?

Such thoughts could be fatal. The fate of my village had to be addressed at another time. I ground as much corn as I could. Once again, I built a fire although I found the state of Seeing I had achieved before more elusive after having eaten Uncle's jerky.

I ate cornmeal and drank water until I became sleepy. I went inside the Stone House, intent on following Uncle's instructions down to the last detail. Whatever his plan and my misgivings, my life was still in his hands as long as I depended on him for so much. Two thoughts occurred to me. The first was, *No Dreams tonight.* The second was, *I must find a knife and learn how to use it!*

~

I AWOKE to the howling of wolves. I rose to see the sky ever more faintly illuminated by the star-cloud. Uncle's instructions pounded in my mind. I put on my tunic, drank some water, and walked down to the Medicine Hut in the darkness. It seemed strange that I was supposed to leave footprints. I waited outside the hut for the first hint of dawn. When the wolves finally stopped howling, I looked up at the stars. As the new star-cloud faded, it made many thousands more stars visible. I thought about who made all of those stars. Had they killed anyone when they were made?

At that question, I saw a streak of red tear between the land and the sky in the east.

I entered the Medicine Hut. As promised, the vase glowed green on the shelf to the right of the door, giving the interior of the hut a dream-like hue. I took the vase in my right hand, as instructed. As I held it, it began to burn my skin, but the burn was not like that of a fire. It felt as though my hand was melting into the vase. I walked over to the table.

As promised, the bowl on the table began to glow as well. Its light was a slightly more bluish color. I opened the pouch of herbs with my left hand as instructed. I poured the liquid from the vase into the bowl. As I did so, the glow of the bowl became more intense and white in color while the vase ceased to glow and burn my hand. I put the vase down next to the bowl and poured the contents of the pouch, taking care not to spill anything. As carefully as I could, I placed the pouch next to the bowl, whose contents began to boil and produce a cream-colored gas that spilled over its sides and onto the floor of the hut. At that point, I followed the last of Uncle's instructions and left the hut, my feet beginning to burn at the touch of the smoke. I ran back up the path to the Stone House, feeling the smoke chasing me as there was a burst of light behind me .

As soon as I reached the Stone House, I closed the elk-skin flaps at the door and all of the windows. I placed bags of corn and jerky onto the bottom of each of the door flaps to keep out the smoke and sat in the darkness of the house as bright light spilled through the cracks of the skin flaps. Curiosity was driving me mad. I was about to move aside the flap on the window when I heard Uncle's thought, *Don't touch it, Redcloud! It might blind you.*

I sat and waited and ate. Eventually, I slept. Blissful, dreamless sleep.

IT WAS difficult to tell what time of day it was when I arose because the light I had created continued streaming through the curtains. I took the time to eat more jerky and drink more water. For as bright as it was, the interior of the house was quite cold. I bundled up in the bearskin blanket Uncle used in the winter. I wondered how I could remember certain things over others. How could I remember that Uncle (my habit of calling him that was becoming less irksome) used the bearskin, but I could not remember how he raised me, or how I got here, or even how old I was?

Based on my rediscovered memory, I must have been quite small when he took me. Although I seemed to know how to pack a punch with those flashes, Uncle must have taught me how to Dream, how to make stars, yet I remembered almost nothing compared to what actually must have happened. I had no House Girl to guide me further. The thought of her caused another knot in my stomach.

*Steady*, I thought to myself. I couldn't afford to harbor such feelings and survive any other encounters I'd have with Uncle and the Mighty-One. I certainly didn't feel strong enough to challenge either one of them. I drank more water, then I went back to sleep.

*Redcloud!* Uncle's thoughts were faint. *This is the last set of instructions I can give you before we must Dream together with the Mighty-One. You must commit these instructions to your memory in the same way you carried out the instructions for the signal. Your actions have been impeccable up to now, and soon, all shall be at peace, Redcloud.*

He continued. *This signal will continue for another day. When it is finished, you must return to the Medicine Hut. The hut itself will be a charred pile of ashes. You must go to the exact center of the circle that made up the floor of the hut. Take a sharpened stick for digging that you will find leaning on the back side of the Stone House. Dig through the ash. If you come across either the bowl or the vase, set them aside. You will bury them outside the circle if you find them. If you don't find them, pay them no mind and continue digging in the center. Eventually, you'll hit the hut's original floor. Keep digging in the exact center until you hit a white rock about a forearm's length beneath the original floor.*

*After you hit the rock, you will pry the rock free. Beneath it, you will find another pouch. Do not open it immediately; its powder will have been cured by the signal fire. You will use it to protect yourself from the Mighty-One's Power when we all Dream together in three days. You will take this pouch with you in the Dreaming Hut we rebuilt for you. Once inside, you will spread this powder all over your body before you begin your Dreaming Song. I will guide you as you meet the Mighty-One, so He may have His new world to conquer. Repeat from the beginning.*

I repeated. I was surprised I found it so easy to remember so many instructions, but he still had me repeat three more times. *In honor of the three days,* he thought.

In essence, he wanted me to wait and do his bidding one more time. Perhaps this could be the last time.

## 24

## VISIONS IN GREEN

It felt like morning when I awoke. There was a bright red hue shining through the crack between the elk skin and the window sill. The signal seemed to have run its course. I rose and peeked through the door to see the whole of the world covered in ash. Bits of white seemed to bounce in the breeze. I sneezed, which disturbed the ash. I sneezed again. I let the flap close. As beautiful as this scene was, I had to cover my mouth and nose.

I searched about the house to find an old piece of cloth we used to wash the dishes. I shook the dust off and held it to my face to cover my mouth and nose. After putting on my tunic and sandals, I ventured out into this painted world.

Every footstep kicked up more ash. It looked like snow but behaved like dust. I walked around the back of the Stone House. This was a trip I had rarely made except to urinate in desperation. Every new movement caused the air to sparkle in the rising sun. I turned around to face the back of the house. I saw the stick Uncle referred to. It was about as long as I was tall and sharpened at its base. As thick as my arm, it had a slight curve to it, but it was very solid. It looked recently sharpened. Was there a knife?

I put the digging stick back, taking care to disturb as little ash as possible. I sneezed again and fell backward. Another cloud of ash caused more sneezing. I rose, and the ash seemed to follow me. Another two sneezes seemed to clear the air in the general vicinity of my face. I slowly walked back inside the Stone House and fiddled with the cloth until I was able to tie it in a knot behind the back of my head and still keep my nose and mouth covered.

I retraced my steps until I had returned to the back of the house. As soon as I approached the digging stick, a brisk breeze arose from the bottom of the hill below. A large cloud of ash passed. I choked slightly as the digging stick and the ground beneath it were swept clean. I walked to pick up the stick, then bent down to look at the ground. Buried in the wild grass next to the foundation of the Stone House, I found some chips of rock. I picked them up and examined them. They were much too small to be used as the knife that would have sharpened the edge of the digging stick. Having no knowledge of this at that time, I tried to carve more shavings of wood off the stick using the rock flakes. After cutting my right pinkie finger open, I stopped.

While sucking on my finger, I rooted through the grass. Finally, I found a flake that was about the same size as the palm of my hand. With care, I attempted to slice the wood on the stick. As slivers flaked off the stick, I knew I had what would be my first knife. I carefully placed it into the pouch I had attached to the rope around my waist.

On my way to the Medicine Hut, I saw a thin layer of ash continued to stick to the surface of most of the plants but was largely absent from the ground, which ceased to have a snow-like quality. I felt like a ghost as I walked with the digging stick.

As promised, only a pile of ash remained of the Medicine Hut. At the time, I could have no understanding of the tremendous loss of knowledge the burning of that hut represented. The ash was darker in color and consistency. It was more dirt-like and didn't blow as easily in the wind. The darker ash pile was remarkably circular. The center was marked by the top of the pile.

Slowly, I began to remove the top of the pile. Some of the heavier ash remained suspended in the air but fell to the ground quickly. As the pile became smaller in size, my hands became blacker and blacker until I reached the midpoint between the ground and the bottom of the pile. Then, the ash became green. As I removed more ash, it became clear that ash had concealed the bottle that had been used to carry the liquid for the signal. As I unearthed this bottle, I remember being curious as to how someone could hollow out such a hard stone. There was something odd but familiar about it beyond my having used it to make the signal. I took the bottle and placed it outside of the circle. I returned to the pile. I kept removing the ash. As I came to the end of the layer of green ash, a sudden burst of wind forced the green ash up into my mouth and nose through the bottom of my mask. Everything became green.

A TONE ERUPTED in my ears. I felt a thud as my backside hit the ground. The greenness began to undulate into shapes as the tone shifted into notes, sliding up and down in pitch. The undulations began to take on shapes: a long tooth, then a tongue, then a mouth. The green tongue licking the green teeth. I heard myself breathing amidst the tone. With each breath a new shape, a second mouth, smaller, somehow more menacing. The first mouth roared a familiar roar as the shape of the Jaguar, my protector, became clear in all his green ferocity amidst the undulations.

The smaller mouth hissed as the body of the Cougar took shape. They began to square off in what would amount to a titanic battle with a certain outcome as the Jaguar was at least twice the size. Again, my breathing caused a shift as the green Cougar slinked off into the clouds of the pulsating green background.

The green clouds behind took on another shape only recently familiar. A low growl in my ears told me I was seeing a village from the point of view of the Jaguar. The village began to fill out in the colors of my memory. This was my village. I felt a shudder deep within my guts at this realization. Another breath revealed warriors in an aggressive posture running toward the Jaguar. I sensed an odd satisfaction as the Jaguar plunged himself into the foliage, seemingly to avoid the pursuit of the warriors en route. As his paws came into view, it was clear that he was much smaller, a cub. The greenery rolled by as the shapes became reminiscent of the green clouds from which the village had emerged. The Jaguar leaped to the top of a boulder as it came into view. I heard two spearheads hit the face of the boulder as the Jaguar took cover behind it. The Jaguar turned its keen eyes back to see two warriors come into the clearing. In shading their eyes from the sun, their breathing became more erratic as they knew the roll of hunter and prey had reversed. Another warrior came into the clearing as the first two recovered what was left of their spears.

"It's gone!" the first warrior shouted in my own

language. It was the first time I could remember any other voice speaking my tongue besides Uncle and myself.

"We chased it away!" called the second warrior.

"Go back then," said the third. "Jaguars almost never hunt people anyway." I felt a pinch of relief at hearing his voice. This caused my breath to deepen making the scene more resonant.

"How would you know? Have you seen one before?" asked the first.

"Only in Dreams," said the third.

"I'm going back," said the second warrior. "We've done our part."

"Yes. Let's go back," said the first as he turned to leave.

"I'll be along," said the third.

"It's not safe to stay," said the first. "We must leave together."

"You go on," said the third. "I feel like there may be something else to see. I'll be back shortly."

"Don't stay long. The sun is setting," said the second warrior as he turned to follow the first who had already started back.

As soon as the first two warriors were out of sight, the third put his nose to the wind and sniffed as an animal does. He sniffed so much that his belly began to glow.

"Where are you?" he shouted as he stopped suddenly. "I can't smell you in the wind."

*You must not be smelling hard enough!*

"My nose is not as strong as yours."

*You must go with your friends, or I'll have to kill you.*

"Perhaps, but I must confess that I lied earlier. I have seen a jaguar before. Only two days ago, in fact. It was large and female. She was dead."

*You saw my mother. She became ill and couldn't keep her territory further south, so she brought me here.*

"She was wise and brave."

*And now, she is dead. I was just learning to hunt! I'm hungry. I've been skulking about you and your foul smelling land! I've been eating scraps!*

"Take care, young jaguar, and take heart. Stay hidden from my people, and I will help you as you learn your way in this new land."

*What do you know of the ways of a jaguar?*

"Nothing." *But I am learning the ways of a warrior. I will teach you as I learn.*

A COUGH and this scene disappeared and flashed back to rolling green. Another sneeze brought a pair of hands into focus from the green soup. More breathing caused the hands to solidify. They were older hands, leathery, that were attached to the body I was inhabiting. They held the jade vase with a stopper. I became aware of a voice singing. I was seeing through Uncle's eyes standing in the Medicine Hut. His Song caused the vase to glow more faintly than it had as I made the signal. I caught my breath, and my perspective zoomed into the bottle, a stony-green view of cracks and crevasses.

As my perspective zoomed out from the bottle, the Song remained the same, but the voice had changed. Pulling farther back, my eyes caught sight of smaller, rounder hands. The voice was silky and feminine. It was the voice I had only heard a few times, the voice of the House Girl. As her singing became more intense, I felt her hand begin to burn as mine had. She looked down at the same bowl I had used to make the signal. It was glowing as it had for me. Then I heard a crack of thunder. The kind of thunder that can only be made by bone hitting bone. The House Girl fell to the side. As she rolled over onto her back, her sight revealed Uncle standing over her with his club in his hand. His eyes glowed white as he reached down to take the vase from her stunned hands. My rage surged as the scene faded back to green ringed in red.

I heard voices and thoughts: Uncle's, the House Girl's, the Jaguar's, others that were soothingly familiar but unrecognizable. "Redcloud!" "Redcloud!" "Boy!" The voices began to overlap as puffs of green revealed heads and faces fading in and out of recognizability. "Young one!" "Redcloud!" "Redcloud!" I felt myself put my own hands to my own ears as I began to Sing one distinct high note ...

... The note persisted ...

... The green came back to the clouds ...

... The clouds turned to white as parts of the green flattened out phasing to blue. I took a breath and continued to Sing the same note until I was able to turn my head and see the ash-covered ground again. I sneezed again followed by a cough whose momentum brought me to sitting.

Another sneeze, as I felt something drip onto my thigh. I untied my mask to see that the inside was covered in a coating of green ash suspended in layers of mucus saturating the cloth rag. Another sneeze brought me to standing. Puzzled, I turned my head to see the jade vase. I remembered Uncle's command to bury it outside of the circle and wondered if that was more for my benefit or his. And what of the pouch at the bottom of the ash? To whose benefit were those contents?

If I were to defy Uncle, I would have to flee completely. Even if I did flee, I could never be safe as long as he was alive. How long could the Jaguar protect me from him? Could he? And what of the Mighty-One? Did the Mighty-One remember me? Could I ever flee from him? Could I ever not flee or not be at the mercy of some protector or other? Could I be free? Free from what? Free to what? I had no evidence that Uncle had ever intended to harm me personally other than to keep me from my memories. I couldn't even be sure if he was directly involved with the death... the death of my family. Did the Jaguar know my family? Why didn't he tell me? I needed answers, not questions. First answer, I had to leave now or go forward with Uncle's scheme. Second answer, if I did not flee now, I had to be prepared to do so at any time. Third answer, if I survived my encounter with Uncle and the Mighty-One, I would need to know more about the Jaguar.

I bathed, I slept. I remember no Dreams of any kind from that night. It was as though my Dreaming Body was as exhausted as my physical body.

# 25

## A WORLD APART

The next morning brought enough hunger and loathing of Uncle's "herbs" that I settled into making a spark shortly after sunrise. The rigors of making the spark caused me to think about escape. Where could I go?

Watching the water in the clay pot reminded me of those burning people in the star world, and my stomach sank. They were just like the people who burned in my village.

*I can't make anymore stars,* I thought. *No matter the consequences of defying Uncle... the Old Man, or the Mighty-One ... the Giant.*

How could I flee when I couldn't even call my enemies by their right names? I felt dejected as I saw bubbles beginning to form on the surface of the water in the pot. The only thing I knew how to do better than either the Giant or my ... the Old Man was to make stars ...

Or was it? I could stay in those Dreams longer and do more in them than I had ever seen Uncle do. I had never seen the Giant in any of those Dreams, even though Uncle kept claiming that the Dreams were to spread his conquest.

If that was true, why didn't he go himself? Why didn't Uncle take him himself? Why did they need me? I must be able to do something in those Dreams that neither of them could do.

The water in the pot had come to a full boil. I used a wooden spoon to scoop the fresh ground cornmeal into the water and stirred it so it wouldn't burn on the bottom of the pot. My memory came alive as I remembered the House Girl doing this very thing. The meal boiled and became thick as I stirred. I used another stick with a hook on the end of it and pulled the pot from its perch atop the leaned-to branches framed above the fire. I placed it gently on the ground next to the fire, then spooned the meal into a bowl to cool it down, just as the House Girl had done.

I remembered watching her as a young boy. She must have enjoyed my reaction to her labor because that was one of the few memories I had of her smiling. It started first in her eyes. Then it spread to her cheeks as they became tight and round, causing her lips to curl. She spooned the meal and looked at me again. She laughed briefly exposing her beautiful teeth. The House Girl ... She smiled at me. She laughed at me ... But she was afraid of Uncle. I knew she was afraid even then, but I didn't know why. I knew his treatment of her was either dismissive as though she wasn't even there or outright abusive, just as in my Vision in Green.

A feeling became unburied again. As much as I depended on him, Uncle, the Old Man, must die. Perhaps the Jaguar could do it in the course of protecting me, but even if that wasn't so, he must die. I could turn him into a star. I could do it some place far from others. As strong as he was, I thought I could do it in the course of his pleasing his Mighty-One. His cruelties to my family, either direct or indirect, were unforgivable. His cruelties toward the House Girl were beyond redemption. And his Giant would have to die as well. These thoughts came to me as Visions in which Uncle ... and the Giant exploded in starlight, never to return.

These dark thoughts consumed me as I ate my cornmeal. I drank water afterward. The liquid seemed to spread resolve to every corner of my being. I looked about the clearing, breathing lightly in the brightness. I took a deeper breath and drank more water.

Another question came to me. Why was the House Girl singing the same Song as Uncle as she held the jade vase in my Vision? If this Vision showed me things as they actually happened, did Uncle teach her the Song, or did she teach him? If Uncle could use the vase to make a signal, then perhaps the House Girl was doing the same when he beat her. Another gulp of water and another breath kept the rage from clouding my mind. If the House Girl could use the vase and the vase's Song as a signal as Uncle ... the Old Man did, then perhaps I could as well.

A maneuver began to formulate in my mind. All must be well between Uncle ... and myself and his ... Mighty-One. I must have no ill will in our gentle plan of conquest. I would do everything I was told. I would enter the Dreaming Hut, as I was told. I would bring Uncle's pouch as I was told. I would open the path to the new lands for the Mighty-One and right after he went, I would attack my Uncle without mercy or warning. I would crush him into a star! If he attempted to defend himself by attacking me, the Jaguar would attack him as my protector. If the Mighty-One attacked me, the Jaguar would attack him as well. If I or the Jaguar succeeded, I would Sing the Song of the Jade Vase which I would bury shallowly right next to the Dreaming Hut itself, bringing me back to my Dreaming Hut. If I should fail, if I should die in this attempt at serving Justice on my Uncle and his Mighty-One, then at least I would die a warrior's death.

~

THEY HAVE TO WIN, *the Dark Creatures,* thought Lourdes. *I've been watching them. I don't know if they are aware of me or not, but if they don't get what they want, you'll be ripped apart like the Giant.*

*Perhaps,* thought Redcloud, his voice trembling.

*I can't let that happen to you,* thought Lourdes. *If we can save the Giant, we can save you.*

*She's right,* a new thought rang through their minds. It was the House Girl. Lourdes' vision altered to Seeing without the need for Song. The three of them appearing as egg-like balls of energy. *I've waited for ages Redcloud. You have to stay intact, so we can start our journey together.*

Lourdes saw a wave of affection emanate from Redcloud's egg. *My love!*

*No time for dalliances, love. We need to save you,* thought the House Girl.

*But how?* thought Lourdes.

*We have to make a world apart. I know the Song, but I'll need help to Sing it, and Redcloud cannot participate. He has to relive his battle with Uncle*

*I can help you!* The thoughts of the Jaguar blasted them as his egg also appeared before them although it sat at a different angle from the others.

*You can start,* thought the House Girl, *but you can't finish. In the end, Lourdes, it will all come down to you. You need to learn the Song for yourself, so we can move on.*

*Me? I'll do everything I can, but I've never done anything like this before. I don't even know how I'm doing this,* thought Lourdes.

*You aren't doing anything, and that's how it's done,* the House Girl responded. *A world apart isn't done, it is. Learn the Song. Be the Song.*

With that, Lourdes heard a manner of music unfamiliar to her. As she took a breath in her bed, a similar tone emerged from her egg.

## 26

# THE FORCE OF WORLDS

I spent the rest of the day making my preparations. I filled my gourds. I buried the jade vase near the Dreaming Hut, and I ate my fill of nuts and meal. As the sun set, I looked at the dying fire mimicking the dying sunlight. This would be, perhaps, my dying day. A sensation rippled over my body at the thought. It was time. I hiked to the Dreaming Hut.

As I arrived, all looked as it should, as it must. I slid inside the Dreaming Hut. As instructed, I opened the pouch and applied the sweet-smelling white powder to my skin until my entire body was covered. I closed my eyes and began to sing the Song of Dreams.

The Song brought my perspective to the moonlit cliff of the Sun Daggers that Uncle had shown me before.

I heard Uncle's voice singing as well. He stood behind the Mighty-One, who was seated with his back toward the cliff. The Giant was so large that even sitting, Uncle's head appeared as a second face stacked on top of his beloved King's. As Uncle's song became more intense, there was a burst of flame that shot up between the daggers. The Giant began singing. His voice threatened to overtake all others. The quarter moon started to grow. The moonlight became brighter as it began to drown out the faded glory of the new star.

I felt myself being forced away from the cliff face as my Song become more strident. The ground below became a pool of light. It was then that I saw a new form come out of Uncle himself. It was the Cougar that Uncle had trapped before he left. Uncle and the Giant hit a note that pierced the sky as the now full moon began to grow in intensity. The glowing ground revealed itself to be a door to the new world Uncle had promised. The ground below the door was charred sand, the aftermath of one of my stars. I then saw the Giant forced out away from the cliff by the combined Power of the Cougar and Uncle. The register of horror and serenity on the Giant's face caught me by surprise as he plummeted into the portal to the Dream world below.

I looked down to see the devastation I had wreaked upon what must have been the remains of the city with the golden statue on top of the stone palace. As soon as I saw the Giant pass into the Dream world, I began singing the Song of Collapse, concentrating my efforts on my Uncle. My betrayer, the murderer of my forgotten family, the murderer of memory itself, his rage at my betrayal was formidable. His surprise at my attack was counterbalanced by his sheer Power. I heard Uncle screech in his Song. My breathing was more regimented as my Song of Collapse became more disciplined.

*You have brought death to yourself and all the world, Redcloud!* Uncle's thoughts pounded the night disturbing my Song.

The Giant split himself below. One of the Giant's bodies forced itself up toward me away from the portal, back into our world. I redirected my Song of Collapse toward the Giant as he recoiled in the terror of submission. He plummeted back into the wasteland below following what must have been his physical body.

"You think you can defeat me?" Uncle's maniacal voice shouted over the din of the screaming moon and stars. He hurled himself at me, his form shifting to that of a massive condor. His talons and beak glowing with deadly speed and force. I then redirected my Song toward Uncle.

I quickened my breath as I quickened the pace of my song. Uncle's assault was blunted as his energy became more diffuse. The sharp edges of his former weapons splaying into strings of energy as his body began to collapse on itself.

*A kernel of corn,* I thought. *A grain of sand,* I thought.

"You killed my family!" I shouted in a voice so large that the mountains shook. "You used my Power to murder innocents!"

As soon as these words left my being, I felt myself being crushed with a force beyond all description. The Giant's Dreaming Body had wrapped its enormous hands around my abdomen. He was squeezing all the life out of me. As I lost my concentration, Uncle's condor re-formed itself and came barreling after me. I focused my energy on the moon of the waking world as I lifted myself and the Giant's Dreaming Body, causing Uncle to hit the Giant with all of his Power. I was free of the Giant's grip of death. I saw that the ground had shifted in the portal below. It was over a vast sea of water! I was blindsided by the energetic equivalent of slashing claws and teeth.

The Dreaming Body of the Cougar tore into me. The stinging was unbearable as my Song faded, the glowing below faded.

"You're out of your depth, boy!" Uncle shouted. Another blow from the Cougar assaulted my Dreaming Body, followed by another blow from the Condor .

"Did you believe you could ever make a star without my guidance?"

Another blow as I felt the powder on my skin in the Dreaming Hut begin to constrict me.

"Did you believe that yours was the only family killed by the Mighty-One? It is my honor to serve. It was my honor to watch my family killed, just as it was their honor to die. It was my honor to kill your family in His service, just as it was their honor to die."

"The only honor in their deaths is that they fought to live Justly," I shouted back. "They fought for their families and their communities. What do you fight for, Uncle? What does he fight for? Your Mighty-One fights for his own glory and nothing else, as though glory could be had by taking it from someone else!"

"Betrayer!" Uncle shouted. "The Mighty-One brings order to chaos. He brings comfort to the fearful by concentrating their fear. He brings peace by making relentless war, and now He will conquer an even greater world than our own!"

"Yes!" The Giant shouted.

With that admonishment, the Cougar dove into the Giant with all his fury.

"A worthy opponent for you, my King! Let the Cougar's sacrifice propel you to glory!"

"To Glory!" shouted the Giant as the ground shifted beneath the portal again to the black island in the black sea.

"Yes! Glory! And you, Redcloud, orphan of the forgotten, the last of the dirt of the old world, now it will be your honor to die. Just as your parents did, you will die at my bidding!" shouted Uncle.

Uncle reared his massive condor beak up into the disk of the newly full moon as the Jaguar came at him from behind and clamped down on his long neck with the jaws of his Dreaming Body. I saw Uncle's form become diffuse. I saw the Giant hurtling down into the charred island of the Dream world as the Cougar's Dreaming Body attempted to devour his immense form. I looked above me as Uncle had regathered his strength and began attacking the Jaguar's Dreaming Body. Now that Uncle's Song was no longer concentrated in my direction, the constriction of the powder had loosened, but I knew I would be at his mercy as long as my physical body was covered in it. I tried to turn myself over in the Dreaming Hut, but the powder wouldn't budge from my skin.

*The water!* I thought. Perhaps I could use the water in the hut, but I would have to summon more control of my physical body while maintaining the portal to the Dream world as the Giant still resisted the Cougar. If he remained here, it would be death to us all.

Then, the worst happened. The Giant defeated the Cougar by ripping its Dreaming Body to shreds, its energy fading into the periphery like sparks bouncing out of a blazing fire. I saw the Giant and his double rise to rescue Uncle from his battle with the Jaguar as the portal to the island of the Dream world began to fade.

*Don't lose the Song!* I demanded of myself, but I had to defend my protector. I began singing the Song of Collapse again. The Giant then redirected his efforts toward me. It was then that I let go of all hope of rescuing my physical body from its powder bonds and focused my song at the Giant himself with full fury. *You murdered my love and now, you must die. A kernel of corn!* As one of his massive bodies began to collapse, panic once again seized his consciousness. He stumbled and recoiled as his second body rejoined his first. My Song became louder, my breath more forceful. *A grain of dust!* His form collapsed in half and in half and in half again when I felt my Song being crushed by the powder. I refocused my vision on the Jaguar's battle with Uncle. The Jaguar had suffered a debilitating blow as his energy began to lose its shape. Uncle's energy was hurtling toward the Giant and me, reclaiming his shape as the Condor. I felt more and more restricted as he got closer and closer.

It was then that it dawned on me. If my physical body was being restricted, I mustn't fight. I must collapse my own body. Not into a star but enough to free myself from the powder. At this realization, I hurled myself toward the cliff allowing Uncle to pass by me and smash into the Giant. The blow seemed to cause him to fall back through the reformed portal. I saw the Jaguar floating in the distance. He was intact but faint. *It is my time to protect you now, my Protector,* I thought.

*Now I am twice indebted,* his thought trickled back.

With no time to consider this response, I began to focus my Song of Collapse into my own physical body. At this redirection, I felt my bones beginning to crumble and the portal below to the Dream island divided into two. I cried out in agony. My call caused some stones to fall from the cliff face. An instinctual breath allowed the solid rock to pass through my Dreaming Body.

*You've found it,* the Jaguar thought. *The stones passed through your Dreaming Body because it is made of energy. If you collapse your physical body, you'll crush yourself to death, but if you allow your physical body to become energy, it can pass through the barrier. You must See yourself and the world as it actually is the same way you did before at the other Dreaming Hut!*

At this moment, a cry of fear and rage emanated from Uncle. His Dreaming Body lost all form but began to glow intensely as he hurled himself toward the Jaguar with such force that I had to refocus my vision.

I couldn't see the aftermath of his maneuver toward the Jaguar. I began the Song of Seeing as I had remembered it some days before. My physical body immediately restored to its normal size as my abdomen began undulating. The Song caused the midsection of my Dreaming Body to glow in response.

Uncle careened toward my Dreaming Body. I dove down toward the Giant and the island as Uncle smashed into the rocks that rattled in their fury at such a violation of their energetic integrity. I kept up the Song of Seeing, breathing in an ever more rapid fashion as my Dreaming Body continued to glow ever brighter. Uncle followed me into the Dreaming portals, at which time I hurled myself back into our world. Upon re-entering , I saw the faded form of the Jaguar. I felt Uncle's resurgence.

It was then that I felt a burst within myself. Uncle was no longer a Dreaming Body, but an egg of pure energy. His physical and Dreaming Bodies were revealed as one energetic essence. My own body was the same. The powder which had restricted me fell to the ground in the Dreaming Hut. It was then that I resumed my Song of Collapse.

As Uncle heard my change in Song, his energy intensified and focused itself on me again. In another parry-maneuver to avoid Uncle's aggression, the portal to the Dream world re-formed and shifted. It now revealed the glass and metal buildings I had seen in Dreams before, but there was no evidence of star-making. I could not take the time to examine the detail as Uncle resumed his attack on me. I moved again. The portal shifted with me as my Song of Collapse missed its mark, leaving Uncle unaffected.

This time, I took the initiative against Uncle and smashed headlong with my own energy. Now that my focus was no longer on avoidance, I was able to concentrate my attack. His egg collapsed at the vibration from the Song of Collapse.

*A kernel of corn!*

He collapsed again as I continued singing.

*A grain of dust!* My fury grew as Uncle's energetic form continued to collapse.

*In half and in half and in half and in half and in half again.*

He was smashed until he seemingly disappeared, but my Song continued. The soup of the night began to undulate at the center of what was Uncle's egg of energy. The portal now appeared to be over some vast body of water. I kept singing as I moved closer and closer to him. I Willed him through the portal as my Song came to a crescendo. He exploded into a star as I was forced back into our world, or was I?

## 27

## AWAKE?

Where was I? Which world was I in? All I knew for sure was that I was alone in darkness. The Jaguar was not near me. The Giant was not near me. Uncle was gone. Justice had been done, but instead of satisfaction, I felt only emptiness and exhaustion. Even though it seemed I had achieved Seeing, I felt as though I was the crudest of practitioners. I longed for home. Now, with no one to guide me, I would be locked into the ignorance of trial and error. It was time. I began my Song of the Jade Vase.

This Song was more mournful and less frenetic than the Song of Collapse or the Song of Seeing. I had the sensation of moving, but movement in what form? How does one move when worlds become manifold?

My movement never revealed the form of the Jaguar. It was only the Jade Vase that could find me a place to call home now. There it was. The Green glow. A place to rest at last. I was so very weary.

~

I ROSE TOO QUICKLY as I hit my head on the top of my Dreaming Hut, only it wasn't. I choked as dust began to fall into my mouth and nose. Another sneeze caused me to hit my head again. I checked my forehead, no blood. I felt about in the dark. My hut had changed shape.

*Where is the Jade Vase?*

I began the Song again. The green glow came shooting through the branches of this much rounder, much dustier hut. The green light showed me an opening. I crawled out into the most bizarre Dream I had ever encountered.

As I crawled out of the dome-shaped hut, I saw the shapes of two people. I immediately ducked my head back inside, but they seemed not to take notice. They must have heard me coughing and sneezing. Why didn't they respond? Perhaps they just arrived as well. Perhaps they also knew the Jade Vase. Maybe they were the House Girl's kinsmen?

There was no way to know but to look. The silence made every move I made echo through the darkness. I peered out again slowly. There they were. They stood motionless. The shadows shaded the opening to the domed hut. I poked my head out further, still no reaction.

I looked to the sky for clues only to see that there was no sky! I was inside an enormous room. The ceiling appeared to be made of metal. If I was indoors, where did the light casting the shadows come from? I crawled out of the hut. The people remained motionless. As I stood, I saw the ground I stood on was only a small piece of this room. The light that cast the shadows came from an intense, white fire burning from the ceiling of the room.

*What Dream is this?* I thought.

I inspected the motionless people. They wore clothes similar to my tunic, but they were newly weaved. They weren't breathing! Were they made of stone? Were they cursed?

*Where is the Jade Vase?*

I looked about in the darkness to see if these stone people were my only companions. I saw nothing familiar; everything was as still as the stone people. The only sound was a strange buzzing noise that seemed to emanate from the fire mounted on the ceiling. I sang the Song of the Jade Vase. Immediately, the room was bathed in a green light.

The Jade Vase sat on a white shelf behind clear crystal, which diffused its light as I sang. The green light revealed black symbols on the white wall to which the shelf was attached. The symbols looked like:

**Carved Jade Vase** Item #:A2679243

**Origin:** Unknown

**Date:** Unknown

**Description:** This vase is the only carved jade vase of this type in the world. It was found on a ridge approximately thirty miles southeast of Chaco Canyon National Historic Park near the Jemez Wilderness area by Lucas Garcia-Bernal in 1975. It was donated by his granddaughter Dr. Lourdes Garcia Smith.

- Los Alamos

Historical Museum

The green light suddenly shifted as the Jade Vase fell through the shelf onto the floor. After that, the world was bathed in harsh, white light and terrible, terrible screeching.

REDCLOUD! thought Lourdes. *I can't sing anymore.*

There was no response. Lourdes determined that she had to take the risk of stopping the Song of the World Apart.

She remained in a Dream, but she felt no presence. Redcloud and his companions were gone, whatever that meant.

*Godspeed*, she thought.

Lourdes had never been so exhausted in sleep, but she knew she had to Sing the Song of Seeing once more. When she found the Song's cadence, the world was once again composed of whiskers of light. She decided to attempt to snap her fingers within her Dream to see if there were any Dark Creatures in her presence. Without knowing how, she snapped, and sparks flew. There were no splotches of dark as before.

*Are they gone?*

She snapped again. This time she saw a string of shadows emanating like a tornado cloud pointing to what must be the ground. Another snap brought Lourdes a bit too close for comfort to the tornado of shadows. There they were. The shadows were connected by the thinnest thread of darkness to a cross of flickering brightness. They appeared to be attached to a church.

Another familiar voice rolled through her thoughts as she fell into a deep, mercifully dreamless sleep.

*Are you the queen?*

# ACKNOWLEDGMENTS

A Brief Statement of Facts (these have changed little from my previous Dr. Lourdes Garcia Smith book):

Every word written in this book is a complete fabrication with the following exceptions:

1.I'm a white dude from the suburbs. While I did spend four glorious years of my charmed life in New Mexico and worked briefly at Taos Pueblo, I am not Native American (or Indian as most Native Americans I have met prefer to be called), and I do not pretend any knowledge beyond my own experience of Native Americans. I did use some material from published folktales of various Pueblo communities gathered about 100 years ago, but most of those tales were gathered by white anthropologists and are viewed with some disdain by some Pueblo communities as I understand it.

2.I could not have written this book without the help of my family, my first readers and my previous collaborators. Thank you to my editor Melissa Prediaux. Thank you Estelle Rodkoff, Ivannia Nolasco, Eileen Sisk, Marcia Bigler, Nate Patrus, Lee Meredith, Catherine Arnold, Donna King, Alex Bellas, Mark Peters and Karen Paramanandam. Thank you also to my wife Weng, my mother-in-law Vicky, my children Nicolas, Makayla, my dad AJ, my mother Ginny and my grandparents Keith & Peggy. You have my undying love.

3.There is an historical figure named Redcloud who bears absolutely no resemblance to my character of the same name other than they are both Native American. I encourage my readers to look up the real Redcloud as my limited reading has revealed him to be one of many over-looked American heroes.

4.There is a place in northwestern New Mexico called Chaco Canyon that has building complexes that somewhat resemble the buildings depicted in this book. The building complexes appear to be oriented to track the sun across the sky. They seem to have been intentionally abandoned. Chaco Canyon is a remote National Park. I encourage you to visit, but be prepared for a long, rough ride to get there.

5.All of the Dreaming sequences and other cosmology used in this book appear in the works of Carlos Castañeda. I do not know how to separate fact from fiction in his work, but the methods he described seemed to be a hell of a mechanism to use in my fiction.

6. I would not have a cover or other amazing artwork were it not for Martin Nibali, thank you!

## ABOUT THE AUTHOR

A. Ryan Bigler traveled 1,500 miles in-utero, criss-crossing the Western United States. He grew-up in the Spiritual Wildlands of suburban Salt Lake City. He's a pan-theist. There is no-such-thing as "no-such-thing". In his 20's, he traveled the world and the US absorbing experiences, writing songs, plays and poems. He earned a BA in Theater Studies from the University of Utah and an MA in Theater and Communications from Indiana State University. As a founding member of The Uncle Eddy Theatre Company (formerly) in Santa Fe, New Mexico, he learned how to write, act, direct and produce plays. As a founding member of the bands "A General Lack of Toast" and "The Wild Humans," he learned how to write, sing, dance and record songs. As a founding member of the Bigler family (Reseda band), he learned how to teach, manage, fix, parent and husband. As a teacher at Olive Vista Middle School in Sylmar, California, he learned how to share his learnings with middle schoolers. As your author, he is learning how to spin a tale so fabulous, you'll ache for more!

Learn more at: aryanbigler.com

## ALSO BY A. RYAN BIGLER

DAY ZERO: A Dr Lourdes Garcia Smith Novel

## THANK YOU!

I am honored that you took your precious time to read my book!

It took me well over a decade to put this book together. I hope to get you another book much faster.

If you want to see more books like this one, the best possible way to support me as a writer is to join my mailing list!

I know it's difficult for many of us. Our inboxes already runneth over, but you'll only get my best, and I'm willing to send your choice of a gift as a token of my appreciation. Please click below to see what is on offer to my beloved readers!

All the best!

Click Here to see your Free Gift Menu!

www.ingramcontent.com/pod-product-compliance
Lightning Source LLC
LaVergne TN
LVHW012048160826
845678LV00014B/2744

*9798840735992*